FIRECRACKER

FIRECRACKER

SHANE BARKER

Deseret Book Company
Salt Lake City, Utah

For Rick and Christy

Library of Congress Cataloging-in-Publication Data

Barker, Shane R.
    Firecracker / by Shane Barker.
    p cm.
    Summary: Although terminally ill with lupus, sixteen-year-old Corey uses his Mormon faith to endure, while his magnetic personality enriches the lives of those around him.
    ISBN 0-87579-353-3
    [1. Lupus erythematosus — Fiction. 2. Terminally ill — Fiction. 3. Mormons — Fiction. 4. Christian life — Fiction.] I. Title.
PZ7.B250566Fi   1990
[Fic] — dc20   90-41678
                                              CIP
                                              AC

Printed in the United States of America

10   9   8   7   6   5   4   3   2   1

Prologue

Sixteen-year-old Corey Everest sat on his mother's bed, calmly tossing a tennis ball from hand to hand. His mother's eyes were red, though she hadn't been crying.

"Nephi, Utah," she said. "You really want to move to Nephi, Utah?"

"I know it sounds goofy. But yes, Mom, I do."

"You know there are other options."

"Not really," Corey reminded her gently. "Not if we want to consider Dad." He dropped the tennis ball and put his arm around his mother's shoulders. "I know it's going to be tough, Mom, but I'm worried about Dad. He needs us to be close to him right now."

Mrs. Everest nodded. It was like Corey to be worried about someone else. She had been divorced from her husband for nearly ten years now. He had moved several hundred miles away to Nephi soon after the divorce, and she had seen him only a handful of times since. Still, they had remained friendly to each other, and he was important to Corey.

"What does your father think of the idea?"

"You know Dad. He doesn't say a whole lot, but I know

he wants us to come." He winked. "I think he misses you, Mom."

Mrs. Everest placed a hand on Corey's knee and looked into his eyes. They were as green as lime Jell-O, and yellow rays spread from the pupil into the iris. The rays were called flashes, and some people said they were a sign of psychic power. She smiled, knowing that Corey didn't have any more psychic power than she did. He *was* very perceptive, though, and he had a talent for smoothing over arguments and sensing people's inner needs. In the years since the divorce, Corey had often been the only bright spot in her life, helping her through times that she wasn't sure she could have handled alone.

Corey was looking at her with the faintest beginnings of a smile. She decided to take one more shot. "There *is* a hospital near Nephi."

Corey spoke firmly. "No, Mom. We've already been through all that. No more hospitals."

"Then there's nothing I can say to make you change your mind?"

"No, Mom."

She had tried. "Well, that's it, then. We'll move to Nephi."

Corey hugged her.

Chapter One

Jeremy Falkner stirred the lump of mashed potatoes on his plate and frowned. "Do you know how bored I am?" he asked, lifting a forkful of potatoes and letting it plop back onto his plate.

Kat Ericksen glanced once around the crowded high school lunchroom as she sampled a carton of warm milk. "No," she said, "but I have a feeling that you're going to tell me."

Jeremy smeared his potatoes into a flat circle like a pancake. "I'm so bored that I spent two hours last night color coding my sock drawer."

Kat wrinkled her nose. "You color coded your sock drawer? I didn't even know you *had* a sock drawer."

"Well, I didn't until last night. But I was so bored that I cleaned out my dresser and made one."

Kat—her real name was Kathryn, though no one but her mother ever called her that—shook her head. A high school junior, she had known Jeremy all her life and was used to his "I'm so bored" speeches. He had a new one almost every day. One time, for instance, he had come to lunch, saying, "You know how bored I am? I'm so

3

bored that I actually spent time cross-referencing my geography notes, and that was the *highlight* of my day." Another time he had claimed that he was so bored that he could have used sleeping pills as pick-me-ups.

Sometimes his speeches were funny, but Kat wasn't in the mood for one today. She tried changing the subject. "We *do* have bowling league tonight," she reminded him.

Jeremy slowly moved his hand from his fork, leaving it standing upright in the middle of his potatoes. "Whoop-dee-do," he said. "Ever since Chrissy moved to Salt Lake, we don't even have a whole team anymore. It's just you, me, Javin, and whoever the cat drags in."

"We're still in fourth place."

"Ooh," he said with mock enthusiasm. "Like that really gives me goosebumps."

"Maybe we could find someone to join the team and give us a real foursome again."

Jeremy offered his best that's-a-dumb-idea-but-I'm-not-going-to-say-so-to-your-face expression. "Find a fourth bowler? Right. We're lucky to get an alternate every week."

"It was just a thought."

Jeremy reached across the table and patted her on the arm. "That's okay," he said. "Having thoughts is new for you, and it'll take a while before you're any good at it."

Kat gave up. She knew that Jeremy was usually just exaggerating about being so bored. But he had a point, too—life in Nephi was as exciting as skim milk. She poked idly at her turkey fajita and wondered if something else was bothering Jeremy. He had seemed unusually preoccupied lately. He moaned and complained about things that really weren't any big deal, and that wasn't like him.

She glanced at him. Jeremy had formed his mashed potatoes into a cone and was carefully placing kernels of corn around it like decorations on a Christmas tree. She couldn't help grinning. She had practically grown up with Jeremy, and they spent much of their time together. Even though she thought Jeremy was cute—he had dark wavy hair and a nice tan—there was nothing romantic between them. She had lived next door to him for as long as she could remember, and kissing him would have been like kissing her brother.

Jeremy was suddenly talking again. "It's five minutes later and I'm still bored," he complained. "I can't wait till Friday."

Kat took the bait. "Why Friday?"

"Because that's the day I get to wash my gym clothes." He took his fork and mashed his pile of potatoes. "Ain't nothing like having something exciting in your life to look forward to. Sometimes I think—" He had spotted someone across the lunchroom. "Hey, who's that?"

Kat followed his gaze. A thin boy with pale skin had just taken his tray and was looking for a place to sit. She shook her head. "I don't know. I've never seen him before."

Jeremy lowered his eyebrows. "A new student at Juab High? People transfer *away* from here. They don't *come* here. Not on purpose, anyway."

Kat studied the new boy thoughtfully. He didn't have the striking good looks that a girl could fall instantly in love with, but he did have sharp, clean features that could grow on a person. He was looking absently around the cafeteria, and after a moment he saw Jeremy and Kat looking at him. He grinned and threaded his way across the lunchroom toward them.

"Hi," he said. "Mind if I sit here?"

Jeremy made some room. "Not at all. Have a seat."

"Thanks." The boy set his tray on the table and sat down. He smiled, looking from Kat to Jeremy and then back to Kat again. "My name's Corey Everest. I just moved here."

"Hi," Kat replied. "I'm Kat, and this is Jeremy."

Corey's grin widened a fraction. His teeth, large and square and a bit crooked, reminded Kat of the Osmonds.

"Kat?"

5

"Well, it's really Kathryn, but everybody calls me Kat."

"Kat." Corey repeated her name a little more slowly this time and nodded his approval. "I like it. It fits."

Kat blushed. "Where did you move from?"

"Pueblo, Colorado."

Jeremy frowned. "Pueblo? I've never heard of it."

Corey spread a square of butter over a roll and took an experimental bite. "It's not very famous. Dolly Parton's tour bus stopped for gas there once and we erected a historical marker. Now what about you guys? Have you lived in Nephi all your life?"

They both nodded. "We hope to repent and do better," Jeremy said. "How come you moved?"

"My dad lives here. He's a plumber. We just moved so we could be a little closer."

"Your dad lives here? While the rest of your family lived in Colorado?"

"My parents are divorced," Corey explained. "They split up about ten years ago."

"And now they want to be close again?"

"It's a long story."

"I'm sure we'll have plenty of time to hear it," Jeremy said. "It's not like we're pressed with things to do around here."

"Sounds like you don't like it here."

"Of course we like it," Jeremy said in his most sarcastic voice. "Nephi is the boredom capital of the world. Do you know how boring it is here? It's so boring that the school motto is, 'I don't know, what do you want to do?' Besides that—"

"—there's not a whole lot to do here," Kat said quickly, cutting short Jeremy's speech.

Corey glanced happily around the cafeteria, obviously unconcerned. "Oh, I don't know. There's always things you can do to jazz things up."

"What do you mean by that?"

"Oh, nothing. But you can always make things fun if you want to bad enough."

"Right," Jeremy said. "Like if we really wanted to make things exciting, we could always sit around in a big circle and watch each other yawn."

Kat suddenly had an idea. "Me and Jeremy are in a bowling league, and we need a fourth bowler for our team tonight. Like to come along?"

Jeremy actually showed a trace of enthusiasm. "Yeah. Do you know anything about bowling?"

"Bowling? Isn't that where you pack around a fifteen-pound ball and wear other people's shoes? Well, not much. But I'm willing to give it a try."

"Great," Jeremy said. "We'll pick you up at six o'clock."

"All right," Corey answered. He grinned. Like he'd said, there were always ways to jazz things up.

• • •

Sitting through an hour-long English class every day was like having your head stuffed with Jell-O. Or at least that's how Javin Trujillo felt about it.

Mrs. Hazelboom was one of the sweetest, most caring teachers ever to stand in front of a classroom. And with nearly thirty years' experience, she certainly knew her business. But even *she* couldn't make Shakespeare interesting. Javin wasn't certain there was a person on the face of the earth who could.

He sighed, then mentally switched off Mrs. Hazelboom's lecture and opened his notebook. "*Hamlet*," he thought absently. "*Telmah*."

It was a habit he couldn't break. Whenever he was bored, he entertained himself by reading words backwards. Most words couldn't be pronounced backwards, and those that could usually didn't make any sense. *America* was a good example. *Acirema* didn't mean anything, but it had a nice ring to it. So did *azzip tuh*, *nomannic*, and *ittanicnic*.

Once in a while he found a real winner — like *star*. *Star* spelled backwards was *rats*. And his personal favorite was *maps*. There just weren't many words that had the flavor and personality of *spam*. Javin grinned. Reading words backwards was a dumb habit, but it did have its advantages: he hadn't missed a word on a spelling test since the first of the year.

Javin sighed again and glanced toward the back of the room. When he wasn't reading words backwards, he amused himself by watching the boy who sat in the back corner. He didn't come to class all that often, but when he did he was usually good for a laugh. The boy had long hair that was as black as midnight and as greasy as if he shampooed with WD-40. His eyebrows looked like caterpillars, and his nose was large and hooked like the beak of an eagle. Besides that, it appeared that his entire wardrobe consisted of faded blue jeans and dingy T-shirts. His name was Edward, though no one but teachers ever called him that. To everyone else it was Ed*weird*. Javin grinned. It was almost like Madonna (*annodam* spelled backwards) or Liberachi. All you had to do was say "Edweird" and everyone in the school instantly knew whom you were talking about.

Javin cast another quick glance at him. Edward wasn't any more interested in *Hamlet* than he was. At the moment, he had a motorcycle magazine spread open on his desk, but he wasn't reading it. Instead, he was chewing on a thick wad of gum and staring blankly off into space.

Javin turned and gazed toward the other side of the room. There was a new kid sitting a couple of seats away. He had said his name was Corey, and he was listening intently to Mrs. Hazelboom's lecture. Javin grinned again. New kids always spent the first couple of days trying to impress the teacher. Javin slowly came to realize that everyone was looking at him.

"Javin?"

"Yes?"

"I asked for your opinion."

Javin suddenly felt uncomfortably warm. Everyone was staring at him, waiting for him to answer. He fidgeted for a moment, then asked, "About what?"

There was a ripple of snickers through the room as Mrs. Hazelboom sighed and turned to another student. "Travis, what about you? Why do you suppose Hamlet acted the way he did?"

Javin's heart was pounding even though he was no longer the center of attention. He felt like a nerd. He hated days like this.

• • •

Jeremy picked Corey up at his home at six o'clock. Kat was sitting in the front seat of Jeremy's rusty 1976 Mustang, and a blonde boy who looked about ten pounds overweight was sitting in the back. Corey slid into the seat beside him.

"That's Javin," Jeremy said over his shoulder. "He bowls with me and Kat."

"Hi," Corey said. "Aren't you in my English class?"

"Yeah," Javin said, pleased that he'd been recognized. "Mrs. Hazelboom's class."

"Javin's a whiz in English," Jeremy said. He met Javin's gaze in the rearview mirror. "You guys still studying *Hamlet?*"

Javin held up the paperback copy of *Hamlet* he'd carried everywhere for the past two weeks. "Yeah. Dull Shakespeare made boring."

Corey leaned forward so that he could be heard by

9

Jeremy and Kat in the front seat. "I heard once that Shakespeare helped to write the Bible."

Kat turned to look at Corey. He was wearing a grey-and-red pullover shirt with a dolphin on the pocket, and his gunstock hair was so neatly combed that each hair seemed to be right in place. Kat realized that she was excited to be sitting so close to him, and she knew that her first impression had been right — his looks *could* grow on you.

She tried to speak naturally. "You think Shakespeare wrote the Bible?"

"*I* don't think he did," Corey corrected her. "It's just that some people do."

Jeremy looked up from the road just long enough to cast a quick glance at Corey through the rearview mirror. "Why would they think that?"

"Well, if you go to Psalm 46 and count forty-six words from the beginning, you know what word you come to?"

"What?"

"Shake." Corey nodded his head solemnly, but he wasn't finished. "Then you start from the end of the chapter — you have to skip the very last word which is *selah* and doesn't mean anything — and go backwards forty-six words. And you know what word you come to?"

Javin took a shot in the dark. "Spear?"

Corey nodded again. "Get it? Shake-speare."

Jeremy looked at Kat with his best there's-another-one-born-every-minute expression, then glanced back at Corey. "And that's supposed to prove that Shakespeare wrote the Bible?"

"Almost. Except there's one more thing. The King James Version of the Bible was mostly translated in the year 1610."

"So?"

"So that was the year Shakespeare turned forty-six."

Jeremy and Kat exchanged glances and then burst out

laughing. Javin joined in with his best imitation of the theme song from "The Twilight Zone"—"Do do do do, do do do do..."

"Hey," Corey said. "I didn't say *I* believed it. I was just telling you what I heard."

"I can't wait to tell that one in seminary," Javin said. "Brother Sanders will love it."

"I can't believe anyone really believes that Shakespeare wrote the Bible," Kat said. "I heard that he didn't even write his own plays."

"That's not the real issue here," Jeremy said. "I can't believe that somebody actually read the Bible closely enough to figure all that out."

The nearest bowling alley was in Payson, thirty miles away, and Jeremy, Kat, and Javin usually didn't say much during the half-hour drive. But tonight Corey kept them alive with conversation, making the miles seem to flash by, and it wasn't any time at all before Jeremy pulled into the parking lot.

The bowling alley was busy that night. A thin haze of blue cigarette smoke clouded the air, and the buzz of conversation and the constant crack of heavy balls colliding with wooden pins made it necessary to speak up to be heard.

"Our team is in fourth place," Jeremy said after everyone had rented shoes and Corey had found a ball. "But last week we were awful. We rolled our worst game of the season, so we need to do lots better tonight."

"Okay," Corey said. "But I've got to warn you—I'm not very good."

He wasn't just being modest, either. On his first roll he released the ball so late that instead of gently kissing the floor, the ball sailed high in a long arch. It smacked hard on the boards and rolled into the gutter. Kat winced.

Corey turned around with a grin. "Oops."

"Is it my imagination," Jeremy said, trying to hide a

smile, "or have you got bowling confused with the shot put?"

"I don't know," Corey replied. "But I'm glad the ceiling isn't any lower than it is."

"Try releasing the ball a little closer to the floor," Kat suggested. She got up from the bench. "Here, let me show you." She walked up to Corey and showed him how to stand. "Now, when you begin your stride, just let the ball swing back like this. And remember to bend at the waist like this when you roll it."

Corey did as he was told and managed to hit one pin. He whirled around and punched at the air like a football player who had just scored a big touchdown.

"One," Jeremy said, dutifully recording the score.

"Yeah," Corey said, "but that's the hardest one of them to hit." He looked around. "Okay, who's up?"

"Javin."

"Okay, then, Javin buddy. Show us how it's done."

Javin got into the act, strutting up to the lane with the arrogance of a peacock and drilling nine of the ten pins on his two rolls.

"Good job!" Corey said, slapping him on the shoulder. "Way to knock 'em down."

Kat stepped up to bowl next and was surprised to find Corey standing right behind her.

"No pressure now," he said, whispering in her ear. "You don't feel any pressure; you don't feel any pressure at all." He reached up and began massaging her shoulders.

Kat looked quickly around to see if anybody was watching, then swatted him away. "*What* are you doing?"

"Just trying to get you relaxed."

"Get out of here!"

Corey scrambled back to the bench and clapped his hands. "Okay, now, Kat. Here we go, here we go."

Kat checked to make sure Corey was back on the bench where he belonged and then rolled a strike. She clapped her hands. "See, it helped," Corey said. "You've just been too tense."

When Jeremy stepped up to bowl next, Javin leaned over to Corey. "Watch his curve ball."

"His curve ball?"

"Jeremy's one of the best bowlers in the league," Javin explained. He rolls a curve that'll make your hair stand on end."

Corey watched. And he found that Javin wasn't kidding. Jeremy put so much spin on his ball that it zoomed clear to the gutter, teetered precariously on the edge, then curved back into the pins at the last instant. He knocked down eight pins on his two rolls.

"All right, Jeremy!" Corey shouted. "What a curve, what a curve! Okay, who's up next?"

Corey kept up his stream of chatter and encouragement through the whole game, acting as if each roll meant the difference between winning and losing the world championship. It was annoying at first, but the more Jeremy, Kat, and Javin became used to it, the more they enjoyed it. In fact, it wasn't long before Kat and Jeremy joined in too. And Javin didn't open his copy of *Hamlet* once all night. All three bowlers were so loosened up by Corey's light-hearted approach to the game that they each bowled their best game in several weeks.

"I think," Jeremy said as they drove home, "that we've found a fourth bowler for the team."

"Yeah," Kat said, excited by the idea for more reasons than one. "You want to join us?"

"Sure," Corey said. "Sounds like fun."

The four teenagers passed high fives around the car.

• • •

At school the next day Corey ate lunch with Kat and Jeremy. For the first time in as long as Kat could remem-

13

ber, Jeremy didn't have an "I'm so bored" speech. And he wasn't playing with his food, either.

Instead, he was laughing with Corey and having a good time. "I know a kid named Scott who's a real goofball," he said. "And *he* had a friend named Tom who got lined up on a blind date. Well, the girl had never seen Tom before, so Scott drove over to her house a few minutes before Tom was supposed to pick her up, told her he was Tom, and took her out." He laughed. "Boy, you've never seen *anyone* as mad as Tom was."

Corey laughed. "So what did the girl do?"

"She didn't know what to do. She didn't find out till the next day. She'd had a great time with Scott, but she was also pretty mad that he'd led her on and lied to her all night. She never went out with either one of them again."

"She probably never went out on a blind date again." They both laughed.

Kat spoke up. "I don't think that's funny at all. She probably spent a lot of time trying to make herself look nice for a date that turns out to be a big practical joke."

Jeremy and Corey exchanged glances and tried to look penitent, but neither one of them could keep from grinning. Corey tried to avoid further reprimand by pointing across the lunchroom and changing the subject.

"Who's that guy over there?"

Jeremy looked. "The guy with the greasy hair? That's Edweird."

"Ed*weird?*"

"Yeah. He's the school greaseball. You know, the class burnout, the town hood."

"Really?"

"Sure. He works at the city dump after school. He's a watchman or something."

They watched as Edward dug into a paper sack and pulled out a sandwich. He was sitting by himself at a table on the far side of the lunchroom.

"He looks kind of lonely over there."

"Lonely? Edweird?" Jeremy shook his head. "Naw, he's loaded with friends. The only thing is that they're all in his head."

"I'm going to go over and introduce myself."

Jeremy nearly choked on a french fry, and Kat looked at Corey as though he were crazy.

"Introduce yourself? To Edweird? That's nuts."

"Why?"

"Because then he'd know your name."

"So?"

"So then he'd know who you are — don't you get it? He's the town hood. He probably kills people."

Corey laughed. "He doesn't kill people."

Jeremy cocked his head with the conviction of a person who knew what he was talking about. "I wouldn't be so sure about that. And if he hasn't yet, it's only a matter of time."

Corey just laughed again. "I'll be right back."

He quickly got up and pushed his way through the crowd of bustling students. When he reached Edward's table, he smiled. "Hi, I'm Corey Everest. I just moved here from Colorado."

Edward looked up slowly. His bushy eyebrows lifted just a bit, revealing a pair of blue eyes. He nodded once, then turned back to his sandwich.

Corey didn't give up. "And your name is Ed, right?"

Edward treated him to another thoughtful gaze. He wasn't used to being called Ed. He studied Corey for a moment, then said, "Yeah."

Corey smiled broadly. He pointed to the magazine Edward had spread open on the table. It was dog-eared and covered with crumbs from Edward's sandwich.

"Motorcycles, huh? You own a bike?"

"Yeah. I've got a Yamaha 125." He gazed curiously at Corey for a moment. "You?"

Corey shook his head. "Oh, no. I'm into bowling myself. You like to bowl?"

Edward looked around as if trying to decide if this were some sort of dumb joke. "Bowling?" he sneered. "You've got to be kidding."

"No, it's great," Corey said, holding an imaginary ball up to his eyes. He rolled the imaginary ball down the lunchroom toward a knot of cheerleaders and scored a strike on them. "You ought to come out sometime. You'd be great."

Edward turned back to his sandwich. "Right."

Corey pulled out a chair and took a seat, folding his arms over the table. He noticed that Edward had a thin line of black beneath his fingernails and that his hands were a shade darker than his arms, signs of a mechanic who had washed but not scrubbed his hands.

"You do a lot of work on your bike?"

Edward looked at Corey out of the corner of his eyes. "Some. Had to rebuild the engine."

"You know how to do that?"

"Don't everybody?"

"Corey!"

Corey turned to see Jeremy and Kat waving for him. They were ready to leave the lunchroom. "Well, hey, I've got to go, Ed. Nice talking to you." Edward took a bite of his sandwich and watched thoughtfully as Corey joined his friends and left the cafeteria.

Chapter Two

Even before the move to Nephi, Corey and his father decided that they would spend every Thursday night together. Back in Pueblo they had spent much of their free time together fishing, so they spent Corey's first Thursday night in Nephi fly fishing a stream in the canyon east of town.

As usual, Corey was chattering away as though there was not enough time to say everything he wanted to. "This is a good-lookin' stream, Dad. Looks like there's lots of fish. You come here quite a bit?"

"When I can get away from work." Mr. Everest tucked his pole under his arm and began lashing a tiny fly to the leader. He wasn't any taller than Corey, but his face was weathered and darkened by the sun.

Corey tried casting into a small pool. Even though the sky was cloudy, he was wearing a floppy, broad-brimmed felt hat, sunglasses, and a long-sleeved shirt. It was no wonder he was so pale. "Do you know any of the kids around here?"

"I know a few who live in the ward. And we hire a few boys from the high school to work with us during the summer. How come?"

17

"Just curious. I've been making some friends at school, and I wondered if you knew any of them."

"Who are they?"

"Jeremy Falkner?"

"No."

"How about Kat Ericksen?"

"No."

"Javin Trujillo?"

Mr. Everest thought for a moment. "There's a Frank Trujillo who works at the bank. Could that be his father?"

"Could be." Corey grinned. "Have you ever heard of a kid named Edweird?"

This time Mr. Everest nodded. The corners of his mouth turned up a tiny bit. "You're running around with Edweird?"

"I met him at lunch today. Do you know him?"

"I know *of* him. His father used to be a mechanic at the city shops."

"Used to be?"

"Got fired. I don't know all the details, but it had something to do with being intoxicated while driving a city truck."

"That's too bad."

"I know. As far as I know, he's been out of work ever since."

"So how do you know about Ed?"

"He worked for one of the crews last summer."

"How'd he do?"

Mr. Everest shrugged. "Okay, I suppose. At least they kept him on all summer."

"He told me that he rebuilt the engine of his motorcycle."

"I imagine he could do it. His dad was quite a mechanic. When Ed was on the crew, he was on a truck that broke down one day. The guys were on a tight schedule and needed to get their gear over to another site. And when they couldn't get the truck running, Ed crawled under the hood and got it fired up."

"Edweird fixed it?"

"That's what they said. We razzed the guys quite a bit about needing a high school kid to fix their truck, but apparently he knew what he was doing. In fact — whoa! I think I've got one." Mr. Everest pulled back on his pole, and a moment later he lifted a fish out of the stream.

"Hey, look at that," he said, letting the fish flop onto the grass. "A little brookie. Don't see many of these."

Corey admired the fish for a moment. It was about eight inches long with bluish sides and a white belly. Corey looked up at his dad.

"Are you going to keep it?"

"Oh, I don't know. What do you think?"

"Would you mind if we let them go this time?"

"Not at all." Mr. Everest gently removed the hook and let the fish slip back into the stream. It hung still in the water for a moment as if trying to get its bearings straight, and then darted away. Corey nodded in satisfaction.

They fished until it was dark and then drove back into town for pizza. When they returned home, Corey talked his dad into coming into the house for a minute.

"Mom? Dad's here."

Mrs. Everest walked into the living room. "Hello, Dan."

"Ruth." He gave her a tentative smile. "Did you get moved in all right?"

"Yes, we did. And thanks for finding the house for us, and for all the work you put into it before we arrived."

"Well, I didn't do all that much." He glanced around. "In fact, the downstairs bathroom still needs some tile work done. And you could use new carpet in here. I'll come by this week and take care of it."

Mrs. Everest smiled. "Thanks so much. Would you like to sit down?"

"No. I've got to get back."

19

Corey spoke up. "Thanks for taking me fishing, Dad. It was just like old times."

Mr. Everest smiled. "You bet."

Corey and his mother watched him leave.

"Your father's lost some weight," Mrs. Everest observed.

"I know. But you gotta remember—he cooks for himself. And you remember what his cooking's like."

Mrs. Everest laughed. "Yes, I do. He's the only man I know who needs a microwave oven with a built-in garbage disposal."

"Remember the time he made pasta brick?"

They both laughed about Mr. Everest's one and only attempt at lasagna. All the noodles had clumped together, and he'd tried to defend the inedible result by saying it was a new invention called the pasta brick. From then on, whenever anyone asked what was for dinner, the family joke was to say "pasta brick."

Corey and his mother were both quiet for a moment as they thought back to the time they had been an unbroken family. Mrs. Everest slipped an arm around her son and held him tight.

"How is he handling . . . things?"

"Not so bad, I guess. We didn't talk about it. I think he's trying not to think about it."

"And what about you? How are you doing?"

"I'm okay, Mom."

"Are you sure? Are you still happy that we moved?"

He nodded firmly. "Yes, Mom. I really am. Are you?"

She took a deep breath. "Well, I had my doubts. But yes—yes, I'm glad."

"See, Mom? I said you would be." Corey wagged a reproachful finger at her. "You just gotta learn to trust me."

• • •

On Saturday Mr. Everest came to work on the downstairs bathroom, and Mrs. Everest kept him company as he worked. Corey had gone to an afternoon movie with Jeremy and Javin.

"I wanted to have all of this done before you moved in," he said, chipping away at a clump of old grout.

"You've done more than enough already," Mrs. Everest replied. She felt self-conscious at the formality of the conversation. Even though they had remained on reasonably good terms since the divorce, there was still an awkward distance between them. "I can't thank you enough for finding this house for us."

Mr. Everest rummaged through his toolbox for a screwdriver. "No problem at all. A man I know at the real estate office gave us a good deal. There's not many people moving into Nephi at the moment, so buying homes is a lot easier than selling them."

He unscrewed a fixture from the wall and held it up to the light. "I'm sorry I wasn't able to help you move in. We had an emergency at one of the sites, and I had to spend the whole day on it."

"Don't worry about it. The elders quorum was a great help."

"I knew they would be. They're good men." Because he knew them better, Mr. Everest had arranged for the elders in his own ward, rather than hers, to help them move in.

"One of the men said you were in the quorum presidency."

"I'm second counselor."

"So you've stayed active in the Church, then?"

"I've had a few ups and downs. But yes, I've stayed active."

"That's wonderful, Dan." She watched him work for a moment. "How was Corey when he was with you the other night?"

Mr. Everest put down his tools. "It's hard to say. I kept waiting for him to do or say something out of the ordinary, but he never did." Something occured to him. "Except that he didn't want to keep any of the fish."

"That's his way. He's become sensitive about animals. And he doesn't like to talk about what's happening to him. One of the hospice volunteers in Pueblo suggested that he's going through a denial stage."

Mr. Everest shifted his weight and frowned. "I really don't think that's it. It's not like Corey to turn away from his problems." He took a deep breath. "I suspect that he just doesn't want to burden anyone else with his troubles."

"But is that good? Is it normal?"

"I wish we could all be as normal as Corey." He smiled. "You know how outgoing he is. And he's always putting other people before himself. I suspect that's his way of facing things. The more he hurts, the more outgoing he becomes."

She dabbed at her eyes. "What about you? How are you handling his condition?"

"It's tough. I'm still trying to come to terms with it." He hesitated for a moment and then looked up. "And you?"

She folded her arms and tightened her trembling lips. "The hardest thing is accepting the fact that there's nothing I can do. I keep wanting to believe that there must be something that we've overlooked."

"Me too." He shook his head. "I've never been very prayerful—you know that—but in the last three months I know that I've worn the knees out of four different pairs of pants."

Mrs. Everest managed a smile. It was like her husband to pray only as a last resort. And yet her own prayers had become much more fervent in the past several months as well.

Mr. Everest was just about finished. "I'll come by later

to fix up the carpet in the living room." He looked around. "Is there anything more I can do?"

"Stay close. Please, stay close. I'm going to need your help to make it through this."

He nodded. "I will. I'll come by as often as I can." He thought for a moment, remembering the petty bickering and wanton disregard for each other that had driven them apart. It was all so long ago. He had thought many times since that, given another chance, he would have tried harder to keep things together.

"I know that we've had our differences, Ruth," Mr. Everest said. "We've been through some rough times. But for Corey's sake I think it's important that we put all of that behind us. It's important that we do what we can for him, forgetting our own differences."

She dabbed at her eyes again. "I agree."

He kissed her softly on the cheek as he left.

Chapter Three

Mrs. Hazelboom was standing in front of the chalkboard, trying to generate interest in a poem by Robert Frost. Except for a couple of students in the first row, however, no one was very enthusiastic. Corey raised his hand.

"Yes, Corey?"

Corey stood. "I don't mean to interrupt, but Javin's been making some pretty incredible claims about himself. I was wondering if you could set him straight."

Javin, half asleep in his chair, sat up and began coughing uncontrollably.

Mrs. Hazelboom tilted her head. "How may I help?"

"Well, I know Javin's supposed to be pretty sharp, but he claims that he's the only student in the class who's learned all the poems on the memorization list."

Javin looked around with a wild I-don't-know-what-he's-talking-about expression.

"Anyway," Corey continued, "I thought maybe you'd let us see whether he's right or wrong."

Mrs. Hazelboom was peering at Corey with a look of amusement. For the first time all hour, she had the attention of everyone in the room. Even Edward was looking up from his motorcycle magazine. She nodded. "What did you have in mind?"

"We could test him. We could even make a game out of it." He pursed his lips and thought for a moment. "For instance, we could make Javin stand in the front of the room and take turns giving him phrases from poems on the list. Then Javin has to give us the next line, along with the title and the author. If he can't do it, then whoever stumps him gets to drop a quiz score."

Everyone in the class, including Mrs. Hazelboom, was instantly enthusiastic. Except for Javin. He was staring at Corey with a look of panic. Corey grinned at him. "And if nobody can stump you, then *you* get to drop a quiz."

Javin was terrified, but with everyone egging him on, he timidly got to his feet and walked to the front of the room.

"I'll go first," Corey said. He gazed at the ceiling for a moment and then said, "Okay, here's a good one. Listen close. 'The gazer watched from aspen hills—'" He nodded. "Now finish that!"

Javin calmed a little. He knew this one. Mrs. Hazelboom had composed it herself, and he had taken extra pains to memorize it. He began speaking:

The gazer watched from aspen hills, filled with snowy white;
The wind and cold no contest against the starry night.

He grinned and finished the piece.

For the deep, coal vault like parody of December far below
Held its captive starry specks like frozen flakes of snow.

He beamed. "'Once upon a Starry Night,' by Mrs. Hazelboom."

Mrs. Hazelboom blushed as the class applauded. Then a girl in the front row raised her hand. "I'm next," she said. "'The pedigree of honey—'"

Javin relaxed, feeling confident now. This wasn't as bad as he'd thought. His voice rang out:

25

The Pedigree of Honey
Does not concern the Bee—
A Clover, any time, to him,
Is Aristocracy—

He breathed a sigh of relief. " 'Pedigree,' by Emily Dickinson." Javin successfully completed two more poems before he was stumped when a girl named Marsha asked him for a line from Walt Whitman. According to Corey's rules, Marsha had won the contest, but the class wasn't ready to quit yet.

"It's Marsha's turn now," someone yelled out. "Let's try to stump her."

Mrs. Hazelboom had been trying all semester to get her students excited about reciting poetry, so if that was what they wanted to do, she wasn't about to stop them. She nodded and motioned for Marsha to go to the front of the class. For the next ten minutes the students took turns shouting out lines of poetry. And for the first time all year, they were enjoying the memorization list.

● ● ●

Javin was talking a mile a minute. "I can't believe you did that to me! Talk about being on the spot! I *never* get up in front of a class like that! And reciting poems? I can't believe you made me do that!"

Corey just laughed as they walked to their lockers. "Oh, come on, Javin. You were great! And you have to admit, it was a lot more fun than listening to a lecture."

Javin opened and closed his mouth several times like a fish out of water. Finally he glared at Corey. It was impossible to argue with him, not just because he was stubborn, but because he was right. "Okay. So it was fun. But why did you have to pick on me?"

"Because you were half asleep. You needed a good shot of adrenaline."

"It *did* wake me up. But next time you might try Edweird or somebody."

Corey's expression turned thoughtful. "You know, that's not such a bad idea."

Javin's eyes bulged as if they might pop. "Edweird? You'd really try to get Edweird to stand in front of the class and recite poetry?"

Corey thought about it for another moment. "Well, that might be a bit much. But we should try to get him a little more involved." He looked at Javin. "Is he a member of the Church?"

"I very seriously doubt it. The Church *does* have standards, you know."

"Maybe he's just inactive."

"And probably very happy with the situation, too."

Corey looked surprised. "You don't think Edweird would like church?"

Javin looked back with an expression of astonishment. As bright as Corey seemed sometimes, the most obvious things often went right past him. He tried to sound sarcastic. "No, I think Edweird would feel right at home at church—but only if they had a Sunday School class for motorcycle gangs."

Corey laughed. "I don't know how anybody could live in a town called Nephi and *not* be Mormon."

"It happens more than you think," Javin said, noticing the determined look in Corey's eyes and wondering what he was thinking. He wasn't sure that he wanted to find out.

• • •

On Wednesday Jeremy picked up the gang as usual for bowling league. When they reached Corey's house, Corey bounded across the lawn carrying a bowling bag.

"What's that?" Javin asked. "You go buy yourself a bowling ball?"

"You bet. You guys have all got your own. And I had so much fun last week that I thought I'd get serious. Wait till you see it." He unzipped the bag and pulled out the ball. It was glossy white, painted to look like a huge eyeball.

Kat wrinkled her nose as if she had just taken a look at something old and moldy. "Ick," she said. "Where in the world did you find that?"

"I bought it at the pawn shop," Corey said proudly. "Only cost four dollars."

"Did you pay the four dollars," Jeremy asked, "or did they pay *you* four dollars to get it out of the store?"

"Hey, you can laugh all you want. But wait till you see it knockin' down pins."

"I don't know," Javin said. "I don't think this is what they mean when they say to 'keep your eye on the ball.' "

Even so, the ball was an instant hit at the bowling alley. Bowlers from opposing teams went out of their way to examine it up close and to watch Corey bowl with it. Corey responded to the attention with a constant stream of jokes and stories, and there was a crowd around him and his friends all night.

"Is it me," Jeremy whispered to Kat at one point, "or are we suddenly popular?"

Kat looked around. It was Corey and his bizarre bowling ball that were attracting the attention, but their lane was suddenly the place to be. Bowlers from all over the alley were coming to talk and pass the time between frames.

Kat shook her head. "I don't know," she said. "But don't complain. This is the most fun I've had bowling in months."

Not only that, but it was one of her best nights, too. She started the game with a spare, rolled a strike, then hit two more spares before her arm began to tire and her scores dropped a little. Jeremy and Javin were doing just as well. And even Corey—he wasn't exaggerating when he said his new "eye ball" would knock down pins—was doing well for a beginner. After the game, Jeremy drove to the Burger Barn for ice cream.

"We were awesome tonight," Javin said, stirring a thick strawberry shake. "If we keep bowling like we did tonight, we could take the league championship."

Two weeks ago Jeremy and Kat would have laughed at him, but now they were as enthusiastic as he was. Once Corey was given a handicap, their team scores were bound to get even better.

"You know what, though?" Corey asked, looking over the rim of his cup. "I bet we could be even better."

Jeremy held his straw up to the light and frowned at a chunk of banana that had become caught inside. "What have you got in mind?"

"Uniforms."

"Uniforms?"

"Well, matching shirts anyway," Corey said. "We could put our names on them."

"How would that make us better bowlers?" Kat asked.

Corey sat up straight and assumed his most businesslike manner. "It would give us more pride as a team. It would give us more confidence."

Javin nodded approvingly, but Jeremy wasn't so certain.

"We'd look kind of silly, wouldn't we?" he asked. "We'd be the only team to have them."

"That's the beauty of it," Corey said, feeling his excitement build. "It would set us apart. We'd be great."

"Hmm," Jeremy said. "It's worth thinking about, I guess." He suddenly grinned, wondering what Corey was going to come up with next.

• • •

The next day, Jeremy and Corey were riding home from school together. Kat had left early with a few of her girl-friends, and Javin was staying late to retake a Spanish test.

"Well, what do you think?" Jeremy asked unexpectedly.

"About what?"

"About Kat. Think she's fun?"

Corey nodded vigorously. "Yeah. She's great."

"So why don't you ask her out?"

"Me?" Corey asked in surprise. "I thought *you* liked Kat."

"I do. But not like that."

"Why not?"

"Kat's too much like a sister to me. I've lived next door to her since we were two years old." He laughed. "We lived so close and spent so much time together that I think I was about five before I realized that she *wasn't* my sister."

"And you don't date?"

"Well, not each other. We do a lot of things together, but it's really not like we're dating. We both go out with other people."

"So why do you want me to ask her out?"

"You like her, don't you?"

"Sure I do."

"Then take her out." He lowered his voice a notch, as though he were divulging a closely guarded secret. "I just happen to know that she likes you."

"Did she tell you that?"

"No, but I've known her since I was two, remember? I *know* her. I've seen the way she looks at you. So believe me — she *likes* you."

Corey nodded thoughtfully. And as soon as he got home, he went for the phone.

"Hi, Kat? This is Corey. Would six o'clock be okay?"

"Be okay for what?"

"To pick you up. I'm going to take you out for ice cream."

Kat laughed. "Sure. Come on over."

"Okay."

Corey borrowed his mother's van and drove to Kat's house. When she answered the door, he tucked her arm securely into his elbow and ceremoniously escorted her to the van.

"Here you go," he said, opening the door with an exaggerated flourish. "Watch your step."

He helped her step into the van and then ran around to the other side and hopped into the driver's seat. Kat was smiling.

"You were serious, weren't you?" she asked.

"About what?"

"About taking me out for ice cream."

"Yes, I was."

She laughed. "Until just this second I thought it was some kind of joke."

He looked at her solemnly. "I never joke about gorgeous women."

"Ooh," she said. "I think I'm going to like this."

Corey drove to the Old Malt Shoppe, bought a couple of sundaes at the drive-through window, then drove out of town and up the canyon. It was still an hour or so before dusk, and the sweet smell of pines scented the air. Corey parked in a clearing next to a shallow stream. He spread a blanket over the grass, and they both sat down.

"It's so pretty up here," Kat said, tasting a dainty spoonful of melting strawberry ice cream. "And it smells so fresh."

Corey nodded his agreement. "I think I'd rather spend time in the mountains than anywhere else I know." He shoveled a massive spoonful of raspberry ripple into his mouth. "You know what always amazes me?"

"What?"

He pointed with his spoon. "Look at that hillside over there. Look how many different shades of green there are."

Kat looked. The hillside rose sharply against the darkening blue of the sky. It was blanketed with stands of pine, aspen, and maple, and it blazed with myriad shades of green. In some spots the aspens appeared almost golden, while nearby strips of pine seemed practically black. "It's beautiful," she said.

"Yeah." Corey looked around, drinking in the peaceful surroundings. "There was a place like this in Colorado. I used to go fishing there." He gazed into the distance, picturing the narrow, peaceful canyon. "Anyway, I got some really bad news a few months ago. It was so bad that for a time I didn't think I would ever be able to stand it. But then I'd go up the canyon, and just being there made me feel better."

He looked at Kat. "It probably sounds kind of silly, but being there made me feel closer to my Heavenly Father. It made me realize that everything was going to be okay."

"It doesn't sound silly," Kat said. "Being in the mountains makes me feel the same way." She took another taste of ice cream. "What was the bad news?"

Corey shrugged. "It's not important. I got it worked out." He changed the subject. "Have you ever heard of alpenglow?"

"No."

Corey became excited. "It's great. When you're in the mountains, right after the sun goes down but before it gets dark, everything suddenly starts to glow. It's weird. For a few minutes everything turns golden orange and just glows."

Kat cocked her head. "Really? I've never heard of it before—and I've been in the mountains quite a bit."

"It happens really fast," Corey said. "And it's kind of subtle, so unless you're watching for it, you don't notice it. I never even noticed until my dad pointed it out to me once when we were fishing."

"Do you think we'll see it tonight?"

Corey looked around. "I don't know why not. The higher up in the mountains you are, the better it is, but I think we're high enough to see it here." He gazed up the hillside with an expression that Kat thought was almost reverent. "Alpenglow's one of my favorite things. Seeing it reminds me of everything that's good in the world. It makes me feel good." He looked around for another moment, then slowly came to realize that Kat was peering at him. He grinned. "What are you looking at?"

"You."

"Why?"

"No reason. You're just special, that's all."

He managed to hide a blush. "Why do you say that?"

"I don't know. You just are." She leaned over and studied his face. There was a faint burgundy flush to his pale cheeks that she'd never noticed before. It was shaped like a butterfly and looked like the flush a person sometimes gets after exercising, though it seemed somehow more permanent.

"It's no wonder you like it up here so much," she said suddenly.

"Why's that?"

"Your eyes. They're green, just like everything else up here."

He laughed. "They *are* kind of funny looking, aren't they?"

"They're not funny looking. It's just that I've never seen eyes that were quite that color before. And they have yellow streaks in them."

Corey nodded. "Yeah. Those're called flashes. An old superstition says that people who have them are psychic. But that's just an old wives' tale."

"Psychic, huh? Try to guess what I'm thinking."

Corey assumed his most telepathic expression. He closed his eyes and pursed his lips, trying to look mysterious. After a moment he lifted an eyelid. "I think I've got it."

"What?"

"You're thinking that I'm the best-looking guy that you've ever been out with, and you wish that I'd come closer so that we could hug and kiss."

"You're right," she said softly.

Corey's eyes opened wide. "I am?"

Kat nodded. "Yeah, it must be an old wives' tale. I wasn't thinking anything like that."

"Nothing like—" He threw a handful of leaves at her. She threw a handful back, and the next instant they were throwing leaves back and forth. She tried to stuff a handful down his shirt, but he twisted away.

"Now that's not fair," he shouted. "That's—" He broke off in midsentence, and his face took on the same reverent expression he'd had before. "Look," he said. "It's happening."

It took a moment for Kat to realize what he was talking about. And then she saw it. The mountains and everything on them—the trees, the rocks, the grass—had taken on a marvelous orange hue that made them seem to glow. Even Corey seemed to have a strange, golden radiance about him. Kat wouldn't have noticed the alpenglow unless Corey had pointed it out. The scene was as beautiful and mysterious as he said it would be.

And then, suddenly, it was gone, and the mountains became dull and grey in the waning light. It was several moments before Corey said anything.

"Did you see it?"

Kat nodded. "It was beautiful."

"I told you it would be."

Chapter Four

Corey was standing in front of the class, holding up a finger in his most Shakespearean pose and staring at some obscure point on the back wall.

" 'To be, or not to be,' " he said, reciting Hamlet's famous soliloquy the way he'd seen Sir Laurence Olivier do it on video,

> *that is the question:*
> *Whether 'tis nobler in the mind to suffer*
> *The slings and arrows of outrageous fortune,*
> *Or to take arms against a sea of troubles,*
> *And by opposing end them.*

He paused in his performance and turned slightly so that he was facing the class. His thoughtful expression had not changed, but there was a mischievous twinkle in his eyes.

"Did you know that Shakespeare once thought about writing music?" he asked, abruptly breaking character.

Spellbound by Corey's performance, Mrs. Hazelboom was taken by surprise. She shook her head.

"Oh, yeah," Corey said, as seriously as he could. "In

fact, the first time he wrote *Hamlet*, it was 'Tuba, or not tuba.' "

The class roared, but Corey was suddenly back in character again:

> *To die, to sleep;*
> *To sleep, perchance to dream. Ay, there's the rub,*
> *For in that sleep of death the dreams that come*
> *Must give us pause.*

Corey was not quoting the soliloquy exactly, but nobody seemed to mind. He was so convincing as he spoke that even Mrs. Hazelboom was mesmerized by his performance. For a moment it was as if Hamlet himself were standing before the class, pondering the mysteries of death.

But Corey didn't give anyone long to enjoy it. He broke character again. "You know, after he gave up music, Shakespeare thought about going into medicine. So for a while, Hamlet was going around saying, 'Tibia, or not tibia.' "

This time even Mrs. Hazelboom laughed. She would have preferred that Corey simply deliver Hamlet's speech the way he was supposed to, without the asides. But it was clear that Corey had learned his lines better than anyone else in the class. Besides that, he knew how to deliver them with care and feeling.

And the class was enjoying Corey's antics. He was trying to be entertaining without carrying his silliness too far. She appreciated him for that, and as long as he was putting a little life and energy into an otherwise tedious exercise, she saw no reason to stop him.

Corey was suddenly Hamlet again:

> *The dread of something after death,*
> *The undiscover'd country from whose bourn*
> *No traveler returns, puzzles the will,*
> *And makes us rather bear those ills we have*
> *Than fly to others that we know nothing of.*

His voice died away, and he stared for a moment through the window as if seeing it for the first time. He spoke so naturally that Javin, who was watching from the back of the room, wondered for a moment if it was Hamlet, and not Corey, who was speaking.

Corey suddenly turned and bowed to the class. Everyone applauded, and two or three students whistled shrilly. Corey grinned and waved as he walked back to his desk, hamming it up like an actor accepting his first Academy Award.

Javin gave him a high five and then slapped him on the back. "Good job, Corey. That was great."

Corey just smiled. "Thanks."

"You did that very well, Corey," Mrs. Hazelboom agreed. "Now maybe you could give us an interpretation."

"What?"

"What do you think Hamlet was saying?"

Corey cocked his head. Everyone in the class was watching him, knowing that he was likely to do or say something outrageous. "A lot of people don't agree on what he meant," he said, "because his speeches sometimes contradict themselves. But you know something? I think that Hamlet had the same fear of death that most of us do."

"What fear is that?"

Corey thought for a moment. "The fear that you died," he said, "and nobody noticed."

• • •

Mr. Everest picked Corey up after school.

"Did you have anything in particular planned for this afternoon, Dad?"

"Not really. I thought we could go out for pizza and then to a movie or something."

"Can I make a suggestion?"

"Sure."

"Let's go golfing."

"Golfing? I didn't know you golfed."

"I don't. Do you?"

"No."

"It'll be great then! We'll rent a couple of clubs and balls and go whack 'em around the golf course."

Mr. Everest wasn't instantly enthusiastic. "What about the sun?"

Corey pulled his floppy fishing hat down low over his ears. "Not to worry, Dad. It'll be just like when we went fishing. I'll wear my hat and sunglasses, and I've got sunblock, too. And I'll wear a long-sleeved shirt. And I'm supposed to exercise lots, too—remember? C'mon, Dad, please?"

Mr. Everest tried to look unconvinced, but he couldn't quite keep a straight face. "Okay, then. Sounds like a plan."

They drove to Hobble Creek Golf Course in the canyon east of Springville and rented clubs and balls.

"I have no idea how to do this," Mr. Everest said as he lined up for his first shot.

"Me either," Corey said. "But if we knew what we were doing, it wouldn't be as much fun."

Mr. Everest reared back and swung as hard as he could. He missed the ball completely.

"I don't mean to be critical, Dad, but you see that little white ball? The object is to hit it toward that flag down there."

"Very funny." Mr. Everest stepped up to the ball again and gave it a solid smack. It zipped low over the grass and rolled about fifty yards. "Hmmm," he said. "When they do this on TV, it usually goes farther than that."

Corey pushed a tee into the grass. "I'll bet you a malt I can hit mine farther than yours."

"You're on."

Corey's swing was about as elegant as a baboon attempting a pirouette. But he nevertheless managed to hit the ball, driving it about ten yards farther than his father's. "All right. You can make that malt caramel-banana, please."

"Would you be interested in double or nothing?"

"Absolutely."

"And I'll even spot you the ten yards you already have on me."

"It's a deal."

Mr. Everest approached his ball, selected a club, and sent the ball whizzing down the fairway. The ball landed just short of the green. "Okay, bucko! Let's see you beat that one."

Corey tried to look worried. "Good shot, Dad. It's gonna be hard to beat." He whacked the ball as hard as he could, chopping a divot the size of a softball out of the grass. The ball sliced off the fairway and into the stream.

"Very nice," Mr. Everest said. "Do you get extra points for hitting it into the water?"

"Absolutely. It's considered one of the sport's more difficult shots."

Mr. Everest hit the green with his next shot, but it took him five putts to get the ball into the cup. Corey's next shot, meanwhile, sailed past the green and into the trees on the other side. Mr. Everest cleared his throat. "I don't mean to be critical, but the object is to hit the ball into this little hole over here."

"Cute, Dad. Real cute." Corey found his ball, got it onto the green, then got down on his hands and knees and used his club like a pool stick to knock the ball into the cup.

"We spent twenty minutes on this hole," Mr. Everest observed. "It's a good thing it's not busy tonight or we'd have people stacked up behind us."

"Oh, it'd be good for them. Folks don't get to see world-class golfers like us every day."

"That's true." Mr. Everest was about to tee off on the second hole when Corey stopped him.

"Let's make this a speed round."

"A speed round?"

"Yeah. Neither one of us is any good anyway. So instead of counting strokes, we'll race. We'll both tee off at the same time, and the first one into the cup wins."

"You think you can outrun me?"

"With my golf clubs tied behind my back."

"You're on."

"All right, then. On your mark, get set . . ." Without waiting for "go," Mr. Everest swung, knocking his ball straight down the fairway. He slung his golf bag over his shoulder and began running.

Corey looked up in alarm. "Hey! Cheat! Cheat!" He quickly smacked his ball, then tossed the driver aside. He grabbed a 5-iron out of his bag and sprinted down the fairway. His ball didn't fly as far as his father's, and because he was faster he was the first to get off a second shot. He followed it onto the green and was about to hit it when his father's ball came rolling by. Corey gave it a playful swat with his club, sending it spinning toward the stream.

"Hey! You can't do that!" Mr. Everest charged onto the green and kicked Corey's ball off into the trees before dashing after his own. Corey followed him into the rough, pushing him past his ball and trying to kick it out of the way. Mr. Everest responded by tackling his son and tickling him. Corey fought to get away, finally escaping when his father became tired. They both lay back on the grass and laughed.

"Oh, my," Mr. Everest said, holding his side and trying to catch his breath. "You're crazy."

"I get it from you."

"No, it must come from your mother."

"Then what did I get from you?"

"Good looks, of course."

"That was nice of you, Dad."

"Why?"

"Because you didn't keep any for yourself."

Mr. Everest reached out and grabbed Corey in a headlock. "None for myself, huh? You know what that means —"

Corey twisted under his father's weight and tried to wiggle away. He tried to sound horrified. "You're going to rub my nose!"

It was an old game. Whenever the two of them wrestled — which they did just about whenever they were together — they never went for a pin. Instead, they tried to rub the other's nose in the grass, carpet, floor, or whatever happened to be under them. Because he was so much heavier, Mr. Everest usually won. But tonight Corey was determined to change things.

Slipping out of his father's grip, he flipped over and grabbed Mr. Everest around the shoulders. "I've got you now, old timer! I've got you now!"

"Old timer?" Mr. Everest began fighting back with renewed intensity. "We'll see who's an old timer!"

The two rolled over and over in the grass, laughing and tickling and struggling to gain the advantage. Corey was just about to go for the "rub" when a golf ball ricocheted off a tree and hit the grass, missing them by just a few inches. Corey and his father looked at it for a moment, then burst out laughing.

"There's somebody out there who golfs as bad as we do," Mr. Everest said.

Corey looked at his father. "We ought to hide his ball."

"We could put it in the stream."

They both laughed until a pair of elderly golfers came in search of the ball. The older men studied the Everests thoughtfully before one of them asked, "Are you going to tee off?"

41

Corey pointed at his dad. "I almost rubbed his nose. He's already teed off."

Rather than finish their game, the Everests walked off the fairway and took a seat on a bench.

"Whew," Mr. Everest said. "I can't remember the last time I laughed so hard."

"Me either."

Mr. Everest gazed for a moment at the leafy hillsides — Hobble Creek was one of the most scenic golf courses in the state — and then took a deep breath of the sweet canyon air. He looked at his son. Corey had pushed his hat back on his forehead, and he'd removed his sunglasses.

"You feeling okay?"

"Yeah, Dad. I'm fine."

"Sure?"

"Yeah, Dad. I'm fine." This time there was a crack in Corey's voice, and his eyes began to water.

Mr. Everest became worried. "What's the matter?"

"I'm okay, Dad. It's just that I'm having so much fun. I've missed you so much, and I've wanted to do things like this for so long."

"But?"

"But it's not going to last, is it?"

Mr. Everest put an arm around his son and held him close. "No. I don't think it is."

It was a long time before they left.

Chapter Five

The engine of Jeremy's car was covered with oil and grease and looked as though it hadn't been touched by a mechanic in years. Jeremy wiggled a wire, then yelled, "Okay, try it again."

Corey turned the key in the ignition and mashed his foot down on the gas pedal. The engine sputtered to life, belching a great cloud of blue smoke from the tail pipe at the same time. The whole car shuddered.

"Okay, let off the gas!" Jeremy shouted.

Corey lifted his foot from the pedal and the car instantly died. Jeremy shook his head in frustration. He was supposed to take Kat, Javin, and Corey to a movie in Payson, but when he'd tried to start his car, it had coughed and sputtered like a wild creature about to die. He'd managed to nurse it as far as Corey's house, hoping that either Corey or Javin would know how to get it running again. Unfortunately, his friends knew less about mechanics than he did.

"I don't know what's wrong," Jeremy said finally. He wiggled another wire — he had no idea what that particular wire did, but wiggling it made him feel useful — and then stepped back. "This is great. Just great."

Kat was standing to the side with her arms crossed. "Couldn't we get somebody to fix it?"

Jeremy glanced at his watch and shook his head. "It's too late," he said. "Shops are all closed, and I don't have any money anyway."

Corey stepped out of the car. "I know somebody who could fix it."

Everyone looked up together. "Who?"

"Edweird."

Jeremy's mouth dropped open, and Kat's eyes looked as if they might pop in their sockets. It was several seconds before any of them could speak.

"Edweird?" Javin said, his eyes wide with disbelief. "You've got to be kidding."

"No," Corey said. "I'll bet you a dollar he can have this thing running fifteen minutes after he opens the hood."

"Sure," Javin said, "but then he'd steal our money and murder us."

Corey ignored the remark. "It's our only choice, guys — unless you want to *walk* to Payson."

"We could always take the bus," Kat offered.

Corey spread his hands. "Why won't you give him a chance?"

Javin had his hands on his hips. "Because they don't call him Ed*weird* for nothing. He's a burnout. He's a greaseball. He's a . . . a . . . "

"A hood," Jeremy said, finishing the thought for him.

Corey didn't snort, but he came close. "Listen. Ed's none of those things, and you all know it. If you'd just give him a chance, then A, the car would be fixed; B, it probably wouldn't cost you anything; and C, we wouldn't need to take the bus tonight."

It took several more minutes of arguing until everyone finally agreed to give Edward a chance. They crawled into the car, and Jeremy nursed it toward the junkyard where Edward worked. The car sputtered and trailed thick clouds of blue smoke as they went. Everyone but Corey wondered if they'd still be alive the next morning.

. . .

The only thing that smells worse than an old garbage dump is an old garbage dump under a hot sun, and Kat was certain the smell would cling to her for the rest of her life. She was holding a handkerchief over her face, worried that if she breathed the foul air directly she might catch some exotic disease. As it was, she knew that her hair was already curling from the odor.

A few feet away Corey, Jeremy, and Javin watched as Edward leaned over the greasy engine. He examined the engine for a moment before turning back to his audience. His voice sounded raspy and tired. "Whose car is this?"

Jeremy held up a hand. "Mine."

"You ever give it a tune-up?"

Jeremy looked around uncertainly. "Should I?"

Edward rolled his eyes, then nodded toward Corey. "Hand me that wrench." It was more of an order than a request.

Corey grabbed the wrench. "Here you go, Ed, bud."

Edward gave Corey a sideways glance as he took the wrench and returned his attention to the car. He removed the air filter and began tinkering with something that had a flap and squirted gasoline. He worked at it for several minutes before calling over his shoulder, "Somebody get in and turn it over."

Jeremy crawled into the driver's seat. "Now?"

"Now."

Jeremy turned the key and the car came to life, spurting only a fraction of the smoke that it had before. It rattled for a moment, then smoothed out as Edward made a few more adjustments.

"Let off the gas."

Jeremy took his foot off the pedal. The car continued to vibrate a bit, but the engine was still running.

"Okay," Edward said. "Turn it off."

Jeremy popped out of the car. "It works! It really works!"

Edward wiped his hands on an old rag. "Your plugs are shot, your points are wasted, your timing's off, and your carburetor's filled with gunk," he said, reminding Javin of a television doctor "giving it straight" to a patient. "It'll get you where you're going tonight, but you need to get it fixed."

Jeremy looked properly humbled. "I'll take it to the shop tomorrow."

"That'll cost quite a bit, won't it?" Corey asked.

Edward shrugged. "Maybe eighty, ninety bucks."

Jeremy paled. He had nowhere near that much money.

Corey spoke up enthusiastically. "Why don't you have Ed fix it?" Everyone — including Edward — looked at him as though he were crazy. Corey ignored the stares. "You could do it, couldn't you, Ed? You're as good as any of those grease monkeys in town." He looked at Jeremy. "Besides, Ed'll do a better job than anyone in town, and he won't rip you off like they will." He turned back to Edward for confirmation. "Isn't that right, Ed?"

Edward looked at him uncertainly for a moment and then stared down at the ground. He kicked at a rock and shrugged. "Yeah. I could do it."

Corey nodded happily. "Great! We'll drop the car off tomorrow right after school. And now" — he looked at his watch — "we've got to get going. Come on, guys."

Everyone piled into the car. Corey pushed his head out the window as they drove away. "See you later, Ed, bud! And thanks!"

• • •

After the movie, a comedy starring Chevy Chase, Jeremy

46

dropped Corey and Javin off at their homes and drove Kat to hers. "I can't believe that Corey talked me into letting Edweird fix my car," Jeremy said, holding one arm out the window and steering with the other.

Kat laughed. "I think it's kind of funny. You should have seen the look on your face when Corey suggested it."

Jeremy grinned too. "I suppose I *was* a little bit shocked. I just hope he does a good job."

"He got the car fixed tonight, didn't he? And Corey was right—he had it running in less than fifteen minutes."

"Let's talk about Corey."

"What about him?"

Jeremy shrugged. "I don't know. He's just . . . different, that's all."

"In what way?"

"Well, think about it. How many people do *you* know who go out of their way to make friends with Edweird? And what about that crazy eyeball bowling ball?"

"He just likes being the life of the party," Kat said. "But you know what?"

"What?"

"Things have been different since he moved here."

"Different and dangerous," Jeremy said. "I'm still expecting Edweird to mug me. Maybe I should inform the police."

"Oh, stop it," Kat ordered. "Be serious for a minute."

"I am serious."

"Are not."

"Am too."

She slugged him.

"Okay, okay," he said, clutching his arm and pretending to be hurt. "I'm serious."

"It's just that ever since Corey moved here, things have been different. You never go into your 'I'm so bored' routines, and—have you noticed?—whenever Corey's around, Javin isn't half as nerdy as he usually is."

47

Jeremy thought about it. He had to admit it was true. Since he had met Corey that day in the lunchroom, things *had* been different — and better: Nephi didn't seem quite so dull as it had before. Even his bowling game had improved. Corey didn't bowl well enough to contribute much to the team skillwise, but his firecracker personality livened things up so much that everyone else bowled better.

Still, there was something about Corey that didn't fit, something that didn't make sense. It was a feeling more than a fact, and Jeremy couldn't quite put a finger on what it was. As much as he liked his new friend, he couldn't help feeling that there was much more to Corey than met the eye.

• • •

The next day, Corey went with Jeremy to drop off his car at the junkyard. Jeremy still seemed a little hesitant, but at Corey's prompting he handed Edward the keys. When they picked up the car two days later, they were surprised to find that the engine was no longer caked with grease. Edward didn't seem to think it was any big deal.

"Had to clean it to fix it," he said simply. He handed Jeremy the keys. "Start 'er up."

Jeremy squeezed into the car and nervously turned the key. The engine turned over immediately and purred like a kitten.

"Stomp on the gas," Edward ordered.

Jeremy obeyed. The engine revved up smoothly, without vibrating. There was no smoke from the tail pipe.

"Had a pretty sick car there," Edward said, "but she's fine now."

Jeremy jumped out of the car, grinning from ear to ear. "It runs great," he said. "I can't believe it's the same car."

Corey smiled broadly. "Good job, Ed, bud. Now tell Jeremy how much it's going to cost him."

The grin disappeared from Jeremy's face as he remembered that he still had to settle up. Edward, meanwhile, had pulled a greasy strip of paper from his pocket and was adding figures on it with a pencil stub. It took him nearly three minutes, and from the pained expression on his face it was clear that math was not something that came easily for him. Finally, though, he put the pencil stub away.

Jeremy glanced nervously at Corey.

Edward cleared his throat.

"Thirty-three dollars and ninety-two cents."

Jeremy's eyes popped. "Excuse me?"

"Thirty-three dollars and ninety-two cents," Edward repeated. "And that's firm."

Jeremy looked from Edward to Corey and then back to Edward again. "But—"

"The price is firm," Edward said with a trace of hostility in his voice. "It includes parts and labor, and the job just can't be done for any less than that."

Jeremy shook his head. "No, you don't understand. You said it was going to cost eighty or ninety dollars."

"It would cost you that much in town," Edward said. "*I* don't rip people off."

Jeremy paid his bill, hesitated, and offered his hand. Edward looked at him for a moment, then shook his hand firmly. "Have it checked over once in a while," he growled. "Cars need attention, just like everything else."

"Yeah. I'll do that," Jeremy promised. He glanced once at Corey and grinned. "And thanks . . . Ed, bud."

Chapter Six

On Sunday Jeremy and Corey went to a fireside where a returned mission president urged the audience to invite their nonmember friends to "come unto Christ." After refreshments they went to Corey's house, where they sat on the porch and talked. Jeremy seemed even more preoccupied than usual. Corey tried a joke or two to snap him out of it, and when that didn't work, he tried the direct approach.

"You seem a little quiet tonight. You okay?"

Jeremy looked up absently. "What? Oh, yeah. I'm fine."

"Good, good," Corey replied, obviously unconvinced. He made a guess. "How are things at home?"

Jeremy sat back on the porch. "Not so good," he said. He took a deep breath. "My folks haven't been getting along so well. They don't yell and fight; they just don't seem to like each other anymore." He shook his head and stared off into the distance. "I heard them talking last night, and they're thinking about getting a divorce."

"Wow. That's rough."

"Yeah. It's been pretty tense." He looked at Corey. "I keep wondering if I have something to do with it. I wonder if maybe it's my fault." He shook his head. "I can't help feeling that if I were better, then maybe things would be different. So I've really been trying to do more around the house—you know, keeping my room clean, mowing the lawn, helping with the dishes—stuff like that."

"You can't blame yourself for your parents' problems," Corey said. "You might be the only reason they've stayed together for as long as they have."

"Yeah, I know. But I can't help thinking that maybe if I had been a better son, then things would have been better between them. If they had more reasons to be proud of me . . ."

"You can't start thinking like that," Corey said. "I know— I went through it."

"Oh, yeah," Jeremy said, nodding slowly. "Your parents got divorced when you were what—five or six?"

"Seven."

"Hmm. How did *you* feel?"

"Just like you do. I didn't understand what was happening, but I thought it was all my fault. I remember thinking that my dad didn't love me anymore, and that's why he moved away. It really hurt."

"Did you ever get over it?"

"Not really. I got used to it, but I never got over it, especially since Dad lived so far away. Every time the ward had a fathers and sons' campout, the bishop had to auction me off to somebody." He shrugged. "It's nice that they all went to the trouble, but it's not the same."

"Yeah, I know what you're saying." Jeremy was quiet for a moment. "You know, it's weird—sometimes I don't even want to go home anymore. Not because I don't want to be there—and not because I don't love my parents— but because I don't want to feel like maybe I'm going to do something to make things worse."

Jeremy rubbed at a mosquito bite on his arm. "School's getting to be a drag, too. Things are so messed up at home that I can't study there. And I'm so preoccupied with it all that I can't concentrate in school. I hardly ever know what's going on anymore." He glanced at Corey. "Were you ever like that?"

"No. But then I was just in second grade when I went through it. It's not all that hard to get along in second grade."

"Oh, yeah. That's right," Jeremy said, thinking back to simpler, less complicated times. "Keep your flash cards in order and remember to color inside the lines and you're fine. Boy, those days are sure gone forever."

"Nothing's ever easy, is it?"

"No, it's not." He sighed. "You ever feel like your life is just getting out of hand? Like it's totally out of control and there's nothing in the world you can do about it?"

Corey nodded, knowing exactly what his friend was talking about. "Sometimes you just have to do the best you can and hope for the best." Corey looked closely at his friend. "Can I tell you something?"

"Sure."

"I know what you're going through. I know how much it hurts. But you've got to remember that your parents' problems have nothing to do with you. It's just one of those things."

His voice softened a little. "You're a neat guy, Jeremy. You've got a lot going for you — a lot more than you know. And even though we haven't known each other very long, you're the best friend I've ever had. You really are." He hesitated for a moment. "It's a little like sending you out into a rainstorm and telling you not to get wet, but don't let your parents' problems get to you. Don't worry about it. Just try to hang in there."

Jeremy nodded. Corey had given him a lot to think about.

• • •

On Monday after school Corey borrowed his mother's van and took Kat to Provo for a game of racquetball.

"Have you noticed anything unusual about Jeremy lately?" he asked as he drove.

"I don't know. He's been kind of moody, I guess. Why?"

"Just curious. Just wondered if anyone else had noticed."

Kat smiled. "Did you see the look on his face when you got Edweird to fix his car?"

Corey laughed. "Yeah. He was pretty miffed at me for a while, wasn't he?"

"I'll say. But he changed his mind when he found out how good Edweird fixed his car. Why'd you do that anyway?"

"Why not? Jeremy needed his car fixed and Ed knew how to do it. Besides, Ed needed the attention."

She looked at him closely. "How come you're so worried about Edweird? No one else even talks to him."

"Why not?" Corey asked for the second time. "He's not really as weird as everybody thinks he is. Besides"—he looked at Kat—"I can relate. When I was a little kid, everybody thought I was weird too."

"Why?"

"Who knows? Maybe because I was skinny, maybe because I dressed funny, maybe a lot of things. It got so *I* even started thinking I was weird. So it was nice when somebody would look past all that and give me a chance."

"What happened to change you?"

Corey looked out the window. "Well, my folks sent me to camp one summer. It was the year they got divorced, and they thought it would be good for me to spend a little time away from home. Anyway, there was a counselor there. He was LDS, and he'd just returned from a mission. His name was Jon—Jon Rogers. He was the kind of guy who was always looking on the bright side of things. He never complained about anything."

Corey nodded his head as he thought about his old

friend. "Well, everybody else used to spend all day swimming in the lake. Everybody but me."

"Couldn't you swim?"

"I was afraid of the water. Jon offered to give me lessons, but I was too embarrassed to let the other kids see me."

"So what happened?"

"Not much, except that Jon got up with me every morning at six o'clock—before anyone else was awake—and gave me swimming lessons in the lake." He faked a shiver, recalling the frosty mornings in the ice-cold lake.

"That was nice of him."

"That was nothing. Three months later he had a heart attack. It didn't kill him, but it laid him up for a long time." He looked at Kat. "Can you believe that? He had a heart so bad that it nearly killed him, but he was getting up at six o'clock every morning to give the nerdiest kid in camp swimming lessons."

He took a deep breath, holding it for several seconds before exhaling. "Anyway, to make a boring story short, Jon really made an impression on me, and I wanted to be just like him. So I tried to be happy all the time, I tried to be as good as I could, and I always did things that I thought Jon would do."

"And that's why you're friends with Edweird."

"That's part of it."

"What's the rest of it?"

"I'm not sure. Except if I were Ed, I'd like somebody going out of their way for me."

When they reached the fitness center where the racquetball courts were, Corey changed into a pair of spandex bicycle shorts. They were black with blue leg stripes.

"Ooh," Kat said. "Look at that bod."

Corey modeled for her. He looked about twenty pounds underweight, and his legs were even whiter than his arms. He grinned. "Yeah, this is the kind of body that you'd leave to science fiction."

"Your legs are so—"

"Skinny?"

"Yeah—but they're so *white*."

"I don't get out in the sun much."

"I've noticed that. You're always wearing long pants and long-sleeved shirts."

"Don't forget my hat."

She laughed, picturing the floppy felt hat he often wore. "And your hat. How come you always wear it?"

"Might get sunburned," he replied evasively.

Kat won the first game and was ahead nine to four in the second game when Corey backhanded his racquet into the wall. He gasped in pain, dropping his racquet and collapsing to his knees. He clutched his hand. "Owww!"

"Corey? Are you okay?"

It was a moment before Corey could answer. He was busy flexing his hand, trying to restore the feeling. "Yeah, I'm fine." He winced as a bolt of pain shot up his arm.

Kat knelt beside him and tried massaging his hand. His wrist and knuckles felt strangely lumpy.

"I get arthritis sometimes," he explained.

"Arthritis? Really?"

Corey held up his hand and examined it as if seeing it for the first time. "Yeah. Bummer, huh? I used to think it was something only old folks could get, but I was sure wrong about that."

"Does it hurt bad?"

"I try not to think about it."

Something occurred to her. "How do you bowl?"

Corey smiled. "Like I said. I just try not to think about it. And then when I get home, I soak my hand for an hour in buttermilk."

Chapter Seven

Edward was just sitting down at his usual table for lunch when Corey came bounding over.

"Hey, Ed, bud! You did a great job on Jeremy's car."

Edward looked up with a tired, distracted look on his face. "Thanks." He began opening his brown lunch bag and was amazed when Corey pushed it out of reach.

"Now, I think you'll agree that your skills as a mechanic present us with some interesting possibilities."

Edweird eyed his lunch bag hungrily. "Like what?"

Corey didn't answer directly. Instead, he flipped open Edward's motorcycle magazine and thumbed to an advertisement for a new, top-of-the-line road bike. He tapped it with his finger. "Like that bike?"

Edward nodded. "Sure."

"No — I mean, would you *like* that bike?"

"Sure. Who wouldn't?"

Corey took Edward's lunch bag and started out of the cafeteria. "C'mere and I'll show you how you can get it."

Knowing that he'd have to play along or go hungry, Edward followed him outside to the parking lot. Corey waved his arms. "What do you see?"

"Cars."

"Not just cars," Corey corrected him. "Teenagers' cars. Look at 'em. Half are junkers, and most are owned by kids who can barely afford to keep them full of gas."

"Yeah. So?"

"So most of them aren't in any better shape than Jeremy's. They're falling apart at the seams, and nobody can afford to do anything about it."

"Yeah. So?"

"So you need to go public. Start your own car repair, tune-up, and detailing business. Offer terrific service at terrific prices. You'd have the business of every kid in the school."

"Wouldn't work."

"Why not?"

"No place to work. Not enough tools."

Corey was ready for that. "The school here used to teach auto shop. It still has pits, racks, and probably a lot of tools, too. I'd be willing to bet that you could use them."

"Couldn't afford the rent."

"I bet I could get you the use of the shop every day from three to six o'clock and all day on Saturdays." Corey grinned. "And I bet you wouldn't have to pay a cent for it."

Edward was curious. "How?"

"All you'd have to do is make a deal with the principal. For use of the shop, you'd agree to attend your classes every day and bring your grades up until you have a C average." He spread his hands. "It's easy. Skip a class, lose the shop that day. Fall below a C, lose the shop for good."

Edward wasn't curious anymore. He was interested. "Why would the principal let me do that?"

"For a couple of reasons. First, it would be a service to the student body. And second, you happen to be what people call a 'high-risk' student. They're always worried that you're going to drop out of school and become a menace to society. Principal Harrington would jump at the chance to see you improve from a 'risk' to a solid, C-average student."

Edward wasn't at all offended by Corey's plain talk. He'd heard it all before anyway, so he just asked, "Really?"

"You bet. Believe it or not, Principal Harrington would rather see you earn a C than have a run-of-the-mill kid like me get on the honor roll." He led Edward farther into the parking lot. "Besides that, I might even be able to get you out of a class or two." Now he really had Edward's attention.

"How?"

"Ever hear of work release?"

"Yeah."

"Well, it's kind of like that. Most kids on work release get out of school for a couple of hours to work in the supermarket or something. They get paid, and they get school credit, too. So there's a good chance we can get the principal to work out something like that for you too."

Edward thought that over. In a crazy sort of way, Corey was making sense. Even so, he needed another shot of assurance. "Really?"

"Yes, sir. And the best thing is that you'll get to quit your job at the city dump. You'll make some good money, and if you plan things out right, you could earn enough to buy yourself that new bike."

"You're kidding."

"I'm not kidding. Look, you open a shop, and I bet you could have enough money for a down payment on a motorcycle in six weeks."

All Edward could think of to say was, "You're kidding."

Corey looked wounded. "Hey, Ed, bud, have I ever lied to you? Not only am I not kidding, but I'm telling you that one month after you open you'll be the most slammin', jammin', under-the-hood-and-doin'-it-good auto mechanic in town."

"You really think so?"

Corey put an arm around Edward's shoulders. "Let me put it this way. Your part of the agreement is to have a C average, right?"

"Right."

"Then what are you standing around here for? You've got some serious studying to do."

• • •

Things didn't work out *exactly* the way Corey had said they would. But then, he wasn't too far off, either. Principal Harrington was just as willing to let Edward use the school shop as Corey said she would be, but she did have two unexpected stipulations.

"I want Edward to bring his grades up to C level *before* we allow him to use the shop."

Edward began to panic, but Corey nudged him reassuringly. "Don't worry about it," he said. "We'll take care of it."

Corey then recruited three honor-roll students to help Edward catch up in his studies, offering them free car care for their efforts. Three weeks later Edward completed the last of his makeup work, and the next day Ed's Classic Auto Shop opened for business.

Principal Harrington also insisted that Edward work under the supervision of a faculty advisor. "It's mostly a formality," she explained. She assigned Mr. Saperstein, who had taught auto shop until the program was dropped from the school curriculum, to oversee Ed's work.

Corey also was wrong when he said it would take six weeks before Edward would have enough money for a down payment on a motorcycle. It took four. Kids swamped him with simple repair and tune-up jobs, and they especially liked his detailing business. For ten dollars Edward would wax and polish any car, shining up the chrome and buffing the finish, and he'd apply decal stripes that gave even old, battered cars a stylish look.

It wasn't long before Principal Harrington asked to see Corey in her office. "You seem to have become Edward's personal mentor and business manager," she said, "so I have a matter that I'd like to discuss with you."

"Is there a problem with the shop?"

"Not exactly. I just received a note from Mrs. Hazelboom. Edward's grade in English is dropping again."

Corey nodded in his most businesslike manner. "Did she mention exactly what he's having trouble with?"

The principal handed him a sheet of stiff blue paper. "It's all outlined right here."

"Thanks," Corey said. "Will you give me a couple of days to get this taken care of?"

"Certainly."

Corey went straight to the garage and confronted Edward.

"Look, I've got so many cars in here I spend half my time doing paper work and picking up parts," Edward complained. "I spend less than half my time actually working on cars. I'm spending so much time trying to keep up that I don't have time to study."

"Okay, okay," Corey said, looking for a solution. He snapped his fingers. "Can you afford an assistant?"

Edward answered hesitantly. "Yeah."

"All right, then. I'll be back." Corey went looking for Javin.

"Ed needs some help in the shop," he said. "It'd be worth five dollars an hour for you to run errands and do his paperwork."

Javin liked the idea. He'd learned that Edward wasn't half as weird as everyone thought he was, and his own parents had been after him to get a job anyway.

"There's just one thing," Corey said as he walked away.

"What's that?"

"You need to help him with his English — spelling, poetry, and *Hamlet*."

A few days later Principal Harrington walked into the shop to see how things were going. Edward was hidden beneath a Plymouth Duster, with only his legs sticking out, and Javin was seated at a small table, drinking a soda and jotting figures in a ledger.

"Paroxysm," Javin said.

"Paroxysm," Edward echoed. "P-A-R-O-X-I — "

"Y"

"What?"

"Y — P-A-R-O-X-Y . . . "

There was a muffled reply from beneath the car, followed by "P-A-R-O-X-Y-S-M."

"Good," Javin said. "Now spell it backwards."

"Do I have to?"

Javin took a swallow of soda and nodded, even though Edward couldn't see the gesture. "Yes, you do. That's how I do it, and believe me, it helps."

There was another muffled reply from beneath the car that Edward never would have uttered had he known the principal was listening.

"M-S-Y . . . M-S-Y . . . M-O-U-S-E!"

Javin wrinkled his nose and looked up from his ledger, spotting the principal for the first time. He jumped to his feet, nearly spilling his soda pop over the desk. "Hi."

"Hello." Principal Harrington looked around the shop and nodded in approval. Mr. Saperstein — she'd told him to keep a tight rein on things until Edward proved himself — had assured her that the boys were working out fine. Under Javin's supervision the shop was more orderly than she'd expected. "It looks like you two are keeping busy."

Javin nodded, feeling a twinge of pride that covered his nervousness of having the principal come in for a surprise inspection. "We're offering a ten-percent-off special this

61

week to football players, cheerleaders, and members of Mr. Schary's anthropology class," he said. He lowered his voice and spoke confidentially. "We also offer a standing service discount to anyone in Mrs. Corley's advanced foods class who brings samples."

Principal Harrington smiled warmly. She'd known Javin for two years, and she was pleased to see that he was finally coming out of his shell. Edward, meanwhile, hearing snatches of conversation, rolled out from beneath the Duster to see who was there. He quickly straightened and looked for something to wipe the grease off his hands.

"Hello, Edward. I just stopped by to see how things are going."

Edward shrugged nervously and glanced around the shop. "Things are going okay."

"So Javin tells me. How are your studies coming along?"

Edward looked at Javin, who spoke up quickly. "He's doing great. Watch this." He turned to Edward, and like an animal trainer commanding a dog to do a trick, said, "Spell *lugubrious*."

Edward pinched his lips, uncomfortable at being the center of attention. "Aw, Javin—"

"Do it," Javin urged. "Come on, go ahead."

Edward looked from the principal to Javin and then back to the principal again. "L-U-G-U-B-R-I-O-U-S."

Principal Harrington nodded. "Very good, Edward." She smiled at Javin. "You two keep up the good work."

Javin and Edward watched the principal walk smartly out of the shop. Then they exchanged a round of low fives.

"Good job," Javin said with a sigh of relief. "We impressed the principal."

"And I spelled *lugubrious*," Edward added. "That was my first time."

"Yeah," Javin said with a grin. "Now, spell it backwards."

Chapter Eight

Kat yawned as she left her geography class and walked back to her locker. It wasn't that the class was boring as much as the fact that it was scheduled right after lunch. She yawned again as she opened her locker.

Inside was a paper sack with the words "Rock-em, Sock-em, Razzle-dazzle, Get-lost-in-the-hall-and-meet-a-bigfoot Survival Kit" printed across the front. She grinned and opened the bag. It was filled with penny candy. There was also a note, which read: "I'll never *survive* if you don't go to a movie with me tonight. Corey."

Kat laughed. At least he was original. After school Kat waited for Corey by his locker, and when she saw him, she grinned. "I loved your survival kit."

"You were supposed to. After all, it cost a whole dollar and a half."

"Ooh, big time spender, huh?"

"Well, not really. I just wanted to save a little so I could splurge on you tonight."

"It's a date then."

Corey picked Kat up at seven o'clock and helped her into his mother's van. Kat spent a lot of time with Corey at school and at the bowling alley, but it was still exciting to date him. When they were with other people, he treated her as a good friend. But when they were on a date, he went out of his way to make her feel special. Not only did he make a production of opening doors and helping her in and out of the car, but he stuck to topics she was interested in and didn't dominate the conversation.

Many boys, Kat thought, took her out because they needed a date. She often had the feeling that they were taking her out only because it was a Friday or Saturday night and they were supposed to be with somebody. But not Corey. He made her feel as though she were the only girl in the world.

The movie theater was packed when they arrived, even though they were about fifteen minutes early. They found seats near the center aisle.

"Do you like Harrison Ford?" Corey asked.

"When I was in junior high I had a picture of him in my locker."

"Everybody says this is his best movie ever," Corey continued in his normal speaking voice, which was a notch or two louder than most people were used to in movie houses, "but it can't be better than *Return of the Jedi*."

"Haven't you ever seen *Mosquito Coast*?"

"Well, yeah, but there wasn't a whole lot of action in that one."

"A movie doesn't need action to be good."

"No, but without action, most movies aren't very interesting. Besides, I know why you liked *Mosquito Coast*."

"Why?"

He wiggled his eyebrows. "Because River Phoenix was in it."

She blushed. "That has nothing to do with it."

"No? Okay, why then?"

"Because it was a good movie. It had a good story and was very well directed."

"And you got to see River Phoenix wearing shorts."
She slugged him.

After the movie they drove back to Corey's house and found Mrs. Everest in the kitchen, writing letters to a few of her friends in Pueblo.

"Hi, Mom," Corey said. "I'm going to make Kat a root beer freeze. Would you like one?"

"Only if you can make it without calories."

He thought for a moment and frowned. "I don't think I can do that, but I could make one for you with tomato juice instead of root beer."

Mrs. Everest glanced at Kat, who was wrinkling her nose. "I don't know *how* you can stand to spend a whole night with him."

Kat nudged Corey gently with her elbow. "I just count it as service hours."

Corey tried to look wounded. "Here I am, about to share my world-famous recipe for root beer freezes, and all I get in return is insults."

Kat nudged him again with her elbow. "Oh, we're just teasing."

Corey tried to pout, but his effort only made everybody laugh. Finally he said, "You sit down and talk with my mom. I'll make the freezes."

He quickly dumped a mixture of vanilla ice cream and cold root beer into a blender and whipped it until it was thick. He poured two tall glasses until they were full and then tempted his mother with the rest. "Umm," he said, passing the glass beneath her nose. "Just a little bit left, Mom. Sure you don't want some?"

She glanced at Kat, who laughed and said, "You'd better take it, Mrs. Everest. I know that Corey doesn't like to take no for an answer."

Mrs. Everest studied her son thoughtfully. "Yes, I know. All right, pour me just a little."

Corey smiled triumphantly and poured the rest of the

freeze into a small glass. Kat was already tasting hers. "Umm. Corey, this is delicious."

They talked with Mrs. Everest while they drank their freezes. After Corey drove Kat home, he walked her to the porch, and then, unexpectedly, he kissed her. She was so surprised that she didn't say anything for a moment, but then said, "That was nice."

He nodded. "Yes, it was . . . in an awesome sort of way."

• • •

Mrs. Everest was still up when Corey returned home. "Kat certainly seems like a fun girl," she said.

"She's the best, Mom. She's really a lot of fun."

"Does she . . . know?"

Corey took a deep breath. "No. Nobody does."

"Are you being fair to your friends? They have a right to know."

"I know, Mom. I'm just not ready yet."

Mrs. Everest nodded. The burgundy, butterfly-shaped coloring on Corey's cheeks was becoming more pronounced. She noticed that he was tiring more easily than usual, and she knew his arthritis was troubling him because he often winced while doing simple chores. In addition, Corey moved slowly when he walked, though he never mentioned being in pain.

What worried her the most, however, was the nausea. Corey didn't complain about that either, but when he got up in the morning, she could see by the look in his eyes that he wasn't feeling well. Occasionally she'd suggest that he stay home from school, but he'd perk right up and insist that he was fine.

She hugged him tightly. "You know, the longer you wait, the harder it will be."

He nodded sadly. "I know, Mom. I know."

Chapter Nine

Corey and Jeremy were playing a game of catch football on the lawn behind the high school. Corey was wearing the floppy felt hat he usually wore when he was out in the sun, and his long pants and long-sleeved shirt contrasted sharply with Jeremy's short pants and tank top.

Corey spun the ball in his hands, feeling for the laces, then threw a wobbly spiral. "How are your parents getting along?" he asked.

Jeremy caught the ball with one hand and lobbed it back. "So-so. They've been in to see the bishop a couple of times, and they're going to a counselor."

"Good for them. Is it helping any?"

Jeremy shrugged. "Things aren't like they used to be — and maybe they never will — but at least they're trying."

"How are *you* doing?"

Jeremy shrugged again. "I'm hanging in there. I still wonder sometimes if I'm part of the problem, and that bothers me. And it's frustrating not knowing how things are going to turn out."

Corey nodded. "Yeah, I know what you're saying."

"The worst part is that the house just feels so uncomfortable. Last night after dinner, my folks both went into the den and closed the door. That's no big deal, but I couldn't help wondering if they were talking about me, or them, or the Kansas City Royals, or what. I mean, the quieter it was, the worse I felt. For all I knew, they were figuring out a way to tell me they were splitting up."

"Can make you feel pretty miserable, can't it?"

"I'll say." Jeremy managed an unfelt grin. "I guess I'm getting paranoid, huh? First I tell you things are better; then I tell you how worried I am."

Corey didn't seem bothered by that. "It's natural to be worried. After all, it's your life too. And anything they do affects you."

"Yeah, I know." Jeremy caught the ball and hung on to it. "Can I tell you something?"

"Yeah. Sure."

"Well, I just wanted you to know something." Jeremy hesitated for a moment as he searched for the right words. "This has really been a tough time for me. It's really been, you know, hard."

Corey just listened, not wanting to break Jeremy's train of thought.

"Anyway, I don't want to sound mushy or anything, but I appreciate being able to talk it over with you. It's helped. A lot."

"Sure," Corey said. "Anytime."

But Jeremy wasn't finished. "I wanted to tell you thanks for something else, too."

"What's that?"

Jeremy looked around before he answered. "Well, I've kind of felt a little sensitive about this whole thing. It's not the sort of thing you want all of your friends to know about, and I didn't want anybody else to know about it." He spread his hands. "So I just wanted to say thanks for keeping it to yourself. Thanks for not saying anything to anybody."

Corey nodded. More than anything in the world, he knew exactly what Jeremy was talking about. He hoped Jeremy would remember that.

• • •

Corey took Kat out again the next night. They went to the city park, took off their shoes and socks, and sat in the sand box.

"I'm still worried about Jeremy," Corey said out of the blue.

"Why? Has he been giving you his 'I'm so bored' speeches?"

"No. He's just been a little down lately."

"I've noticed that he's been kind of quiet. Do you know what's wrong?"

"I'm sure it's a couple of things," Corey said vaguely. "But do you know what I've really noticed about Jeremy?"

"What's that?"

"He doesn't have any confidence."

Kat looked up. "Confidence?"

"Yeah." Corey traced his big toe through the sand. "Jeremy is a neat guy. He's smart, he's funny, he's one of the best bowlers in the league, and he has the most incredible curve ball that anyone's ever seen. But he doesn't realize any of that."

"That's true."

Corey pursed his lips and stared up at the sky. The nearest streetlight was out, and he could see the stars clearly. "The problem with Jeremy is that he doesn't give himself enough credit for things. At the bowling alley he thinks more about the pins he misses than the pins he hits."

"And he's like that in everything."

"I know. And the sad thing is that he's one of the greatest guys I know. Everybody likes him. Half the guys in the freshman class wish they were him, and half the girls wish he'd date them. The only problem is that he doesn't know it, or at least he doesn't believe it. What he needs is a little reality therapy."

"Reality therapy?"

"Yeah. He needs a good stiff shot of confidence. That would make all the difference in the world for him right now."

"How do you do that?"

"I don't know. But somehow we've got to convince him that people like him. We've got to give him some good, solid evidence."

Corey thought for a moment and began to smile. It was a smile that Kat had seen before. She said, "You've got something in mind, haven't you?"

Corey nodded and his grin widened. "Yeah. As a matter of fact, I do."

• • •

Jeremy was just sitting down to lunch the next day when Corey slapped a stiff sheet of cream-colored paper down on the table. "Sign this," he said, handing Jeremy a pen.

Jeremy picked up the paper and looked it over. "What is it?"

"An application to run for student-body president."

Jeremy looked up in both surprise and delight. "Student-body president! That's great, Corey. You'll make a great president. You can paint eyeballs all over the school."

"Oh, it's not me that's running," Corey said.

"Well, who is it, then? Edweird?" He looked at Kat and laughed at his own joke.

"No. You are."

"Me? Yeah, right."

"I'm not kidding," Corey said. "Here, look for yourself."

Jeremy snatched up the paper. Sure enough, at the top

70

of the sheet someone had typed JEREMY ALLEN FALKNER. There were already thirty or forty signatures scrawled along the bottom of the application. Jeremy looked up with wide eyes. "This isn't a joke, is it?"

Corey shook his head. "No, it's not," he assured him. "I signed you up this morning. Ten more signatures and you'll be the newest, friskiest, bowlingest candidate for student-body president that Juab High ever had."

Jeremy slapped the application down on the table. "Holy cow, Corey! How could you do this to me?"

"Easy. I just walked into the office, picked up the application, typed your name on it —"

"No! No, I mean, *why* did you do this to me?"

Corey shrugged. "How can you get to be president if you don't run?"

"When did I ever say that I wanted to be student-body president?"

"When did you ever say that you didn't?"

Jeremy opened his mouth to argue some more, but he couldn't think of anything to say. Arguing with Corey was like arguing with a supreme court judge: you couldn't win.

Corey was running a finger down the list of signatures. "Look at who signed this," he said. "Jennifer Paulson, Carey Melton, Bobby Jeffs — these are all popular kids. Andrew Shumway, Bryan Finn, Emily Jacobsen. Can you believe this? They're all *supporting* you."

Jeremy grabbed the application and looked again. "Really?"

"Yeah, really." Corey read a few more names. "Lynette Butcher, Patrick O'Ryan, Clive Cameron."

Jeremy looked up as though he still couldn't believe what was going on. "All these guys really signed this?"

Corey spread his hands. "What do I have to do — beat you over the head with a stick? Yes! They all signed it. They all like you! They all think you'd be a good leader.

They're all going to *vote* for you." Corey took a seat beside his friend and placed his hands on the table. "Listen. You would be a great president. The only thing is that you don't have a lot of confidence. That's why I signed you up. *You* never would have dared to do it."

"Come on," Kat said, voicing her support for the first time. "You'd be a wonderful president."

"Who else is running?"

"Tom Kelly for one. Then a couple of others too." Corey put a finger to his lips. "Let's see, Dana Andrews is running, and Tyler Branon, too, I think."

Jeremy frowned. Tom Kelly probably had the best chance of any of them of being elected. He had a lot of friends, but he also had an ego the size of California. Jeremy had no doubt that the possibility of losing the election would never even occur to him. He pursed his lips and thought it over. Corey's opinion by itself wasn't enough to convince him. After all, Corey had a penchant for strange ideas, even though he was usually right about most things.

He looked again at the list of signatures. They were the most popular kids he knew. He never would have dared ask them to sign a petition, but if they were willing to vote for him — and if Kat was behind him too — well, then maybe he did have a chance. Besides, Corey's endless enthusiasm was starting to rub off on him. Running for president would be an adventure. Even if he didn't win — and he was sure he wouldn't — he'd have a lot of fun. It would be a step out of the ordinary and give him one more opportunity to keep from being bored.

Jeremy looked up to find Corey and Kat watching him expectantly. "Well, okay," he said finally. "Let's run a campaign."

• • •

Everyone met at Jeremy's house the next day to begin work on posters and campaign buttons. Jeremy had only planned on having a few of his friends over to help, but he forgot to take one thing into account — Corey.

"I invited everybody," Corey said when he arrived. "It's going to be great. By the time we're done we'll have enough posters to cover the whole school."

That was the thing about Corey. He wasn't afraid of anything or anybody. He'd go up to people he didn't even know and ask for their help. "We're all meeting at Jeremy Falkner's house tomorrow to make campaign posters," he'd say to someone in the hall. "The whole school's going to be there. Want to come? We're having pizza."

It was something that Jeremy — or most other people, for that matter — would never have dared do. But Corey had such an enthusiastic, outgoing personality that potentially embarrassing situations didn't bother him. And it paid off, too. By the time the poster party was over, there was little need for posters. So many kids were working on the campaign that there was hardly anyone left to advertise to.

"That's the secret of a good campaign," Corey confided. "Getting people involved. The more people we have helping, the better off we are."

The campaign was off to a good start, and soon Jeremy was practically a celebrity. Two days ago he had been just another face in the hall, but now most of the kids flocked around him. They wanted to walk with him in the hall and sit with him in class, and they crowded around him at lunch.

For Jeremy, life in Nephi wasn't dull anymore. And it wasn't just fun. It was exciting.

Chapter Ten

When Corey missed the first three days of school the next week, Jeremy insisted on an explanation as soon as he returned.

"I was sick."

"I called your mom, and she said you were in the hospital."

"The doctor just wanted to run some tests, that's all. So I spent a couple of nights at the hospital in Payson. No big deal."

Corey walked with Javin to English where Mrs. Hazelboom continued the lecture on *Hamlet*. "We have a few minutes left," she said, "and we can spend them reviewing our spelling list, or we can try another round of Name That Poem."

The class shouted out at once. "Name That Poem!"

Mrs. Hazelboom knew which activity her class would choose. Ever since Corey had turned the poetry memorization list into a game, that game had become her most popular activity. The game evolved a little every time they played, and new rules were introduced whenever a new situation arose. "We need to add a new stipulation," Mrs.

Hazelboom had said during their last session. "You can't ask anyone to recite a poem that you can't finish yourself." It was always fun to see what would happen next.

Mrs. Hazelboom called on a girl sitting in the middle of the room. "Melissa? Why don't you be first?"

Melissa stepped quickly to the front of the class. Corey waved his hand. "Me," he said. "Call on me."

"Okay. Corey."

Corey grinned broadly. All right. I've got a good one." He gave Melissa his best ready-or-not look. " 'The sea was wet as wet could be—' "

Melissa jumped right in. " 'The sea was wet as wet could be, you could not see the sea—' " She stopped as several students snickered.

" 'The sand was wet'—no, wait! 'The sea was wet—' " Flustered now, Melissa looked around for help. Then, not finding anyone to save her, she threw up her hands. "Lewis Carroll, anyway," she said as she returned to her seat.

Mrs. Hazelboom looked at Corey. "Can you finish it?"

Corey nodded and recited:

> *The sea was wet as wet could be,*
> *The sands were dry as dry.*
> *You could not see a cloud, because*
> *No cloud was in the sky.*

It's from *The Walrus and the Carpenter*."

"Yes, indeed. You may come to the front of the class."

Corey looked around at the crowd of students gesturing to be called on, then pointed to Rachel Walker. "Okay, Rachel. Try me."

" 'Under the wide and starry sky—' "

The happy grin slowly melted from Corey's face. He stood quietly for a nearly a minute, and it appeared that his mind had gone blank.

Mrs. Hazelboom turned to Rachel. "Rachel, can you finish it?"

Corey spoke quietly. *"Requiem,* by Robert Louis Stevenson."

Mrs. Hazelboom looked at Corey expectantly, but he didn't say anything. "Corey?"

There was a sad, faraway look in Corey's green eyes. He stood for another moment, and when he finally spoke, he whispered:

> *Under the wide and starry sky,*
> *Dig the grave and let me lie.*
> *Glad did I live and gladly die,*
> *And I laid me down with a will.*
>
> *This be the verse you grave for me:*
> Here he lies where he longed to be,
> Home is the sailor, home from sea,
> And the hunter home from the hill.

Corey stood wearing a sad look of melancholy as the bell rang and the rest of the class filed from the room.

"It's no wonder he does Hamlet so well," Javin thought. "He thinks just like him."

• • •

Brother Sanders had the kind face and gentle smile of a textbook seminary teacher. His dark hair was streaked with premature strands of grey, and his eyes sparkled when he laughed. Besides that, he was an excellent teacher. He had a knack for making the scriptures come to life. When he presented lessons on Alma, Moroni, and other Book of Mormon characters, he taught them so well that his students came to know them as real people.

At the moment, he was conducting a scripture chase that was working his class into a controlled frenzy. Students raced through the Book of Mormon, digging out scriptures and waving their hands wildly when they found the right ones.

"Contact! Contact!" Kat yelled, holding her finger down in the book of Nephi. " 'I will go and do the things which the Lord hath commanded.' First Nephi 3:7."

Brother Sanders flashed a hand through the air. "Right!" He pretended to wipe a bead of sweat from his brow and faked a moment of breathlessness. "Whew," he said. "I think that's enough for today."

Corey leaned over and whispered to Kat. "You're the only person I know who does scripture chase at warp three. Do you really use your hands, or do you use the Force?"

Kat grinned happily. "I'm just fast."

"I've heard that from some of the guys you date."

Kat kicked at him across the aisle as Brother Sanders began talking about Alma and Amulek. Corey took a moment to mark a scripture-chase passage he had forgotten about and then looked up.

"Sometimes we need to think about the direction we're going in life," Brother Sanders was saying. "We need to consider our goals and ask ourselves if we have worthy motives." He went on to describe the motives of the priests and lawyers confronted by Alma and Amulek. After a few moments of discussion, a student named Darren raised his hand and subtly altered the subject.

"Alma 12:23," he said. "It says, 'If it had been possible for Adam to have partaken of the fruit of the tree of life . . . there would have been no death.' " He looked up. "Is that true? If Adam hadn't eaten the fruit, then none of us would ever die?"

"Now wait a minute," Brother Sanders said. "You're confusing the tree of life with the tree of the knowledge of good and evil."

"What's the difference?" Darren asked.

Brother Sanders paused thoughtfully, and then he explained: "It was not possible for Adam to eat of the tree of life, but he did eat of the tree of knowledge, and that transgression brought death into the world."

"But would we die if Adam hadn't done that?"

Brother Sanders smiled. "Of course not."

"But why?"

"If Adam hadn't partaken of the fruit, none of us would ever have been born. And if we hadn't been born, then we couldn't die."

The class laughed.

"Actually, Darren has raised an interesting question. But you need to remember that death is as important to us as birth."

"You mean that death is a blessing?"

Somebody spoke up from the back of the room. "It is if you're in Mr. Conway's history class."

Brother Sanders grinned as the class rippled with laughter. "Death is actually nothing more than a passage separating this life from the next step in the Lord's plan of salvation. The reason many people are afraid of it is that they don't understand that there *is* a next step."

A girl named Stacia raised her hand. "So you're saying that death is something that we should look forward to?"

Brother Sanders looked around. "Would anyone like to answer that? Jon?"

"It's not death that's wonderful," Jon said, "but the spirit world is pretty nice."

Stacia seemed hooked on the subject. "What is the spirit world like?"

Brother Sanders knew a teaching moment when he saw one. He reached for his Book of Mormon. "Let's see what the scriptures say. Why don't we all turn to Alma 40" — he waited for a moment as his students opened their books — "and look at verse 6. 'Now there must needs be a space betwixt the time of death and the time of the resurrection. And now I would inquire what becometh of the souls of men from this time of death to the time appointed for the resurrection?' "

He skipped to verse 11. " 'Now, concerning the state of the soul between death and the resurrection—Behold, it has been made known unto me by an angel, that the spirits of all men, as soon as they are departed from this mortal body . . . are taken home to that God who gave them life. And . . . the spirits of those who are righteous are received into a state of happiness, which is called paradise, a state of rest, a state of peace, where they shall rest from all their troubles and from all care, and sorrow.' "

Jon had his hand up again.

"Jon?"

"Isn't that why we're told not to mourn for people who die?"

"It's not that we don't *mourn* for them," Brother Sanders clarified. "When someone dies, we're obviously going to miss them, and it's only natural to mourn their absence. But this is the point—" he said, holding up a finger for emphasis, "we don't mourn their death. That would be like mourning a brother or sister who had graduated from high school and left home to attend college."

Stacia asked an obvious question. "What are spirits like? I mean, how old are they?"

Kat waved her hand. "Isn't it true that all spirits are adults, even if they died as children?"

Brother Sanders nodded. "Not only that, but they are restored to their perfect form." He rubbed the top of his head where he was losing a little hair. "And that's something I can certainly appreciate."

The class laughed. Corey seemed absorbed by the discussion. His arms were folded over the top of his desk, and his eyebrows were pinched together.

"Alma said that people in the spirit world were happy,"

79

someone said. "But what makes them so happy? What do they do all day?"

A boy named Chad said, "They play football!"

Brother Sanders frowned. "They play football, Chad? Without bodies?"

Chad grinned mischievously. "I didn't say it was *tackle* football."

The class laughed again.

"Does anyone have a more reasonable suggestion?"

A girl named Marie said, "Don't they do missionary work?"

"Some do, I'm sure. President Joseph F. Smith wrote that during the three days between Jesus' crucifixion and resurrection, Jesus organized missionary forces to preach the gospel to those who had died without it."

Brother Sanders was making sense, and he had the attention of his class. Kat, in fact, leaned over to make a comment to Corey but stopped before she said anything. Corey's eyes were closed, and his lips were pressed together. For the first time since she had known him, he wasn't smiling.

"Life is short," Brother Sanders continued. "And we all have to die. Death comes into the world to fulfill a merciful plan."

Kat wasn't sure, but it almost looked like Corey's eyes were filling with tears. She tapped his arm. "Corey," she whispered, "are you okay?"

The effect on Corey was electric. His eyes blinked opened, and they weren't their normal green. Instead, they were red and watery.

Kat tightened her grip on his arm. "Corey?"

Corey dabbed once at his eyes and then suddenly picked up his books and, without a word, left the room.

• • •

"Steeeerike!" Javin spiked an imaginary ball and did his version of a touchdown shuffle.

Corey, Jeremy, and Kat all clapped as he strutted down the lane and took his seat on the bench. He crossed his legs and gazed back and forth across the bowling alley like a newly crowned king surveying his empire.

"Jeremy," he said. "I do believe it's your turn."

Jeremy hopped to his feet and went after his ball. All four teenagers were bowling well that night, and with their handicaps they had a good chance of jumping into second place.

"Okay, Jeremy," Corey said. "Good roll, now. Smooth and easy."

Jeremy's teammates sat transfixed as he rolled. No matter how many times they watched him, they still couldn't shake the tension. The ball curved clear to the gutter and teetered dangerously along the edge before finally slicing back into the pins. The pins exploded with a resounding crash. Only two pins were left standing.

"Eight," Kat said with a note of triumph. She penciled in the score as Jeremy dried his hands and waited for the ball to return.

"Easy shot," Jeremy said as much to himself as to his teammates. He took his ball and stepped back up to the line. Javin held his breath as the ball rolled straight for the gutter, loomed over the edge, then suddenly went crashing back into the pins.

"And a spare!" Kat said. "Good job, Jeremy!"

Corey scored eight on his next two rolls, Kat managed a spare, and then Javin was up again. Jeremy left to buy a soda. For the first time all night, Kat and Corey were left more or less to themselves.

"Tell me something," Kat said softly.

"What?"

Kat looked Corey straight in the eyes. "Tell me about seminary this afternoon."

81

Corey's expression didn't change, but his grin didn't fool Kat. It was too forced. He blinked once or twice and looked away. "It was nothing."

Kat spoke quietly but with force. "Corey, don't tell me it was nothing. What's bothering you?"

Corey looked back at her for a moment and then rose from his seat. "I'll be back in a minute," he said, heading for the restroom.

"Nine."

Kat looked up. "What?"

"Nine," Javin repeated. "I got nine."

"Oh, yeah. Nine." She penciled the number in Javin's score box.

"Okay, fine. Don't congratulate me," Javin said.

Kat ignored the comment. "Something's wrong with Corey."

Javin sipped at a glass of soda. "What?"

"I don't know. He's just not acting like himself. Something seems to be bothering him."

Javin shrugged as Jeremy returned. "He seems fine to me."

Jeremy eased into the conversation. "Who seems fine to you?"

"Corey. Kat thinks he's acting funny."

"Corey's always acting funny."

"No, it's not like that," Kat insisted. "He started crying in seminary today. Over nothing. And then he got up and walked out. And when I asked him about it just now, he just got up and left."

Javin and Jeremy exchanged glances. It did sound a little weird, even for Corey, but they had yet to see any evidence for themselves.

When Corey returned a moment later, his face was damp—as though he had been splashing water on it, Kat thought—but he seemed back to normal. He rolled his first ball right-handed and his second ball left-handed, keeping up a nonstop string of chatter the whole time.

Forty-five minutes later the game was over. After their handicaps had been added, they had the highest score of the night. Just as Javin had predicted, the effort moved them into second place.

"We were awesome tonight," Jeremy crowed as they left the bowling alley. "Can you believe it? We're in second place!"

Javin's eyes were wide. "Just think—we could win this thing."

"You bet your booties we could win it," Corey piped up. "And I know how to make sure we do."

"How?"

"The first thing we have to do is get matching bowling balls. You know, like mine."

Kat wrinkled her nose. "With eyeballs? No thanks!"

"Then maybe we could paint them like planets or something." Corey suddenly had another idea. "Hey—we ought to celebrate tonight. Let's go get a banana split or something."

This time his idea was greeted with enthusiasm. The four teenagers piled into Jeremy's car and were off down the road. Corey was still trying to convince everyone to paint their bowling balls when a small dog darted in front of them. Jeremy tried to brake, but it was too late. The car struck the dog with a sickening thud.

Kat covered her face with her hands as Jeremy pulled to the side of the road and stopped. His face was pale, and his hands were wrapped tightly around the steering wheel. He had to ask the question, even though he knew the answer. "Did I hit it?"

Javin nodded. "Yeah, I think so."

Corey looked back through the window and spoke in a whisper. "I'll go look." He quickly crawled from the car and ran back to the crushed animal. It was lying on the side of the road, its chest rising and falling slowly and its eyes open and glazed. Corey gently stroked the animal's head. The dog quivered.

"It's okay," Corey whispered. "Just lie still." He blinked the tears out of his eyes and tried to keep the animal still. It was several moments before he noticed that he wasn't alone.

"How is it?" Jeremy asked.

Corey shook his head. "It's not going to make it. It's hurt too bad."

"I didn't mean to hit it," Jeremy said. "I tried to stop—"

"It wasn't your fault," Kat said, slipping her arm through his and holding him close. "It ran right out in front of you."

"I know, I know. It's just—" He stopped in midsentence. After a moment he nudged Kat and pointed at Corey who was holding the dog with both hands. His shoulders were quivering, and his head was tucked tightly against his chest. He was crying.

"Corey?"

Kat stooped down beside him and put her arm around him.

"Corey? Are you all right?"

Corey shook his head. "It's not fair," he said in a voice that was almost harsh. He rubbed his hands over his eyes, and Kat felt him shudder. "Sometimes . . . sometimes I just can't stand it anymore!"

• • •

No one spoke as they drove home. Javin lived the closest to the bowling alley, but Jeremy purposely drove the wrong way and dropped Corey off first.

Corey's eyes were still red and bleary, but he managed to grin as he got out of the car. "Sorry I was so flaky tonight. I'm just kind of sensitive when it comes to animals."

"Don't worry about it," Jeremy said. "We're all like that sometimes."

"Are you sure you're okay?" Kat asked.

"Yeah. I'm fine. See you all tomorrow."

The teenagers said their good-byes. Jeremy drove around the corner and pulled to a stop. He sat quietly for a moment. Then he looked at Javin and Kat. "Sensitive when it comes to animals?" He shook his head. "I'm sensitive, too, but I can't believe he came apart like that."

Kat nodded. "It's like I said. It's not animals that he's sensitive about. It's death."

"Maybe somebody in his family died," Javin suggested.

"Or maybe somebody is going to die."

The three teenagers looked at one another. It was several seconds before Kat could say what she was thinking. "Maybe it's his dad."

Jeremy nodded his head slowly. "Yeah," he said, "that would fit. That would explain things. Remember when he first moved here? He said it was so he could be closer to his dad. If they're divorced, his mom would never agree to that — unless he really was sick or something."

"Oh, I feel so bad for Corey," Kat said.

Javin wasn't convinced yet. "Let's don't go getting ourselves worked up yet," he said. "All we're doing is guessing."

"That's true," Jeremy said. "But I can't think of anything else that explains things." He looked directly at Javin. "Can you?"

Javin thought for several moments, remembering how Corey had dealt with *Hamlet* and Robert Louis Stevenson's *Requiem*. Both were works about death. He finally had to shake his head. "No, I can't. In fact, all I can do is think up more things that support *your* idea." Javin told them how Corey had been acting in English class. He held out his hands. "It seems like anytime you mention death, he suddenly gets emotional."

"If it were my dad, so would I," Jeremy said.

"I feel so bad for him," Kat said for the second time. "He's the last person to deserve something like this."

"No one *deserves* anything like this," Javin said.

"You know what I mean," Kat answered. She looked at Jeremy. "What do you think we ought to do?"

Javin was ready with a suggestion. "Maybe we should just ask him."

Jeremy wasn't certain that was such a good idea. "I don't know. After all, he does seem pretty sensitive about the whole thing. And if he wanted us to know about it, he probably would have told us."

That was a good conversation stopper. They were quiet for some time. Then Jeremy changed his mind. "I talked some things over with Corey once," he said. "I didn't want to, but he practically forced me to. And you know what? It helped. Talking things over with him really helped."

Kat asked, "So what's your point?"

"Just this. Corey may not want to talk. But if he's at all like me, then he really needs to." He turned and gazed absently out the window. "I think we ought to have a talk with him."

Chapter Eleven

When Corey walked into the living room after school the next day, Jeremy, Kat, and Javin met him with somber eyes.

"Hey, guys," he said, much more cheerful than he had been the night before. "Going bowling or something?"

Jeremy shook his head. "Naw, we were just driving around and thought we'd stop."

"Want some pop or cookies or something?"

Javin looked up hopefully, but Jeremy quickly shook his head.

"No, thanks. We just came to talk."

"Suit yourself." Corey plopped down on the sofa next to Kat and tried tickling her. She smiled politely and wiggled out of reach. Corey looked around. "So what's up? You guys look a little gloomy."

Jeremy and Kat exchanged glances, neither of them certain where to begin. They had planned out what they were going to say, but now nothing they had thought of seemed appropriate.

Corey looked at each of them for a moment. He nodded perceptively. "Aw," he said, "you're here for a talk." He looked at each of his friends in turn. "Okay. Spill it."

Jeremy spoke quietly. "We know about your dad."

Corey's eyes narrowed a tiny bit. "My dad?"

"He's sick, isn't he? We figured it out last night."

Kat slid closer to Corey and placed a warm hand on his arm. "We're so sorry, Corey. And we hope you won't be mad at us for bringing it up like this. But we're your friends. We only want to help."

"Really," Javin said. "You do so much for us, and we just want to help."

Corey looked at each of them in turn. When he spoke, his voice was low. "My dad?"

"That's why you moved here, isn't it?" Jeremy asked. "Your dad is sick and you wanted to be close to him."

Corey still wasn't sure he was hearing right. "My dad?"

"He *is* sick, isn't he?" Kat asked. "We thought he was going to die."

Corey turned and patted Kat reassuringly. "You really are worried about him, aren't you?"

"Of course we are."

"Thanks," he said. "That really means a lot to me."

Javin spoke for the first time in several minutes. "What's wrong with him? Is he going to die?"

Corey shook his head. "No, he's not going to die."

"Then what's wrong with him?"

"Nothing. My dad's fine. So's my mom."

Jeremy, Kat, and Javin all looked at one another uncertainly. "Then who's sick?"

"I am. I've got lupus."

•　•　•

It was several moments before anyone could speak. Jeremy finally broke the spell. "Lupus?"

"Yeah." Corey almost looked disgusted with himself. "It's a disease that usually affects girls. Can you believe that? I won't bore you with all the details, but it's pretty nasty."

Kat whispered, "That's the bad news you told me about, isn't it?"

"Yeah."

"But why didn't you say anything?"

Corey shrugged. "I didn't want anyone to know."

"But why?" Kat asked. "We're your friends! We love you!"

Corey gripped her hand tightly. "I know. But that's why I moved away from Pueblo. People didn't know how to act around me. They couldn't treat me like a friend anymore. All they wanted to do was feel sorry for me."

He looked at each of them. "I didn't want to keep anything from you. I just wanted the chance to be myself. I wanted you to treat me like you'd treat anybody else."

Everyone was thinking the same question, but it was Jeremy who finally found the courage to ask. "Lupus," he said. "Is it . . ."

"There's no cure for it," Corey said. "All you can do is treat the symptoms."

Almost without thinking, Kat blurted, "Why aren't you in a hospital?"

Corey shrugged. "There's really not much a hospital can do. Like I said, all they can do is treat the symptoms, and I can do that myself." He took a deep breath. "The doctors in Pueblo talked about a lot of different medical options, but they all meant spending months in the hospital. They wanted to plug me full of tubes and wires and fill me with all kinds of drugs. A couple of them even wanted to try organ transplants. But they were just grasping at straws. The most they can do is stretch things out a bit. Maybe give me a couple more months."

"But wouldn't even a couple of months be worth it?"

Corey shook his head. "I already spent three months in the hospital in Pueblo. The treatment made me feel worse than the disease, and believe me, it wasn't much fun. Besides, being in the hospital was as hard on my mom as it was on me. She wanted to be with me all the time, so she practically had to live in the hospital lobby."

"That's terrible."

"I know. Being in the hospital is almost worse than being sick. And I want to live as much of my life as normally as I can. That's why I came here."

"But why don't you want anybody to know?"

Corey allowed himself a solemn grin. "Because people are so cruel about the whole thing."

"Cruel?"

"Yeah. They don't mean to be, but they are. They're always saying things like 'If you just had enough faith, then you could be healed.'" He spread his hands. "I've had priesthood blessings—lots of 'em. And I have faith, but I get the impression that people think it's my own fault that I'm sick."

No one knew exactly how to respond to that. There was an uncomfortable moment of silence; then Corey continued. "Back in Pueblo, one lady even asked my mom what we'd done to make the Lord punish us like this. People just don't understand. They don't realize that bad things can happen to good people. Then they're always asking if I'm in pain and how much time I have left and"—he looked at Kat—"why I'm not in the hospital."

Kat reddened and turned away.

Corey patted her on the arm. "I'm only teasing you," he said. "It's just that I get tired of the same old questions all the time. And that's why I came here. I wanted to do my own thing without people always watching me and whispering about me behind my back."

He looked at each of his friends in turn. "I'm sorry if I made you feel like I didn't trust you. But I didn't want you to feel sorry for me. I wanted you to treat me like anybody else." He took a deep breath. "I know what you're all wondering, but after what I've said, you don't dare ask me any questions, do you?"

They silently shook their heads.

"Well, I'll tell you what you want to know. First, except for a little arthritis, there's not a lot of pain involved with lupus. So I'm kind of lucky that way. I've got this funny stain on my cheeks, and I get rashes that look like zits. The sun bothers me too. That's why I've always got to wear that goofy hat. But that's about all there is to it. Sometimes I get dizzy and lose my breath — and sometimes I feel a little sick to my stomach — but it's nothing that really hurts." He tried to smile. "But the biggest question everybody has is how much longer I have left."

They all looked at him without saying anything. He shrugged. "I don't even know the answer to that. No one does. It could be three days, three weeks, three months . . ." He looked a little sad. "Probably not three years." He stared out the window for a moment, and then he looked back at his friends. "I can count on you to keep this a secret, can't I?"

They all nodded solemnly.

"I know what you're all thinking. You're wondering how to treat me, aren't you?"

They looked at one another and nodded.

"Please don't treat me any differently," he said. "Treat me just the way you did before. Treat me like everything is normal."

"It's going to be hard," Kat said.

"I know. But please try."

"I can't believe you can go through this and still be as cheerful as you always are," Kat said. "I'd be miserable."

"If it weren't for you three, I would be," Corey said. "You guys keep me busy, and you make me happy. I cry a lot when I'm alone, especially if I let myself start thinking about it." His eyes reflected a hint of sadness. "But usually I feel like I just don't have any more tears left to cry."

• • •

Later that night, Corey drove Kat to the city park. She was trying to act as normal as she could, but acting was not one of her more obvious talents.

"You feel self-conscious around me, don't you?" Corey asked.

"No."

He looked at her with the expression a bishop might use on someone who was not being totally honest during an interview. She tried to look innocent and then finally nodded. "Yes, I do."

"Why?"

"I don't know. I just don't know what to say anymore. I don't know what to do or how to act."

"That's part of the reason that I didn't want anybody to know I was sick," Corey said. "When I was in Pueblo, *everybody* knew. And everybody felt funny when I was around."

"Are you mad at me?"

Corey took her hand and squeezed it. "No, I'm not mad. I just wish I knew what I could say to make you feel more comfortable."

They sat down in the swings and began swinging gently back and forth.

"How about this?" Corey said finally. "Suppose we were both a couple of years older. And suppose I was going to be leaving on a mission in a couple of days. How would you feel?"

"I don't know. A little lonely, I suppose. But I'd be excited about your mission."

"How would you act around me?"

"Same as always."

"It's really not all that different, you know. Just pretend that I'm leaving on a mission."

"But if you were just going on a mission, you'd be coming back."

"Maybe." He thought for a moment. "What you're really saying is that if I were going on a mission, you'd know that you'd be seeing me again. Right?"

"Right."

"And if I die, you don't think you'll ever see me again?"

Kat looked over at him and tried to make out his features, but in the darkness it was hard to see him clearly. "I never thought of it like that. I will see you again, won't I?"

He nodded confidently. "Count on it."

Chapter Twelve

There were times when Mrs. Everest actually forgot about her son's illness. After all, for the most part Corey seemed to be just like any other young man. He worked hard in school, he spent a lot of time with his father and friends, and he went out of his way to find the fun in life. But when Corey suffered an occasional relapse, she was painfully reminded how fragile life had become for him. Those were the times she turned to her support groups, and her most immediate source of support was the ward bishop.

"You're welcome to call me anytime," Bishop Frost told her. "But let's schedule a weekly visit."

"I don't want Corey to know about it," Mrs. Everest said. "If he knew I was worried, he'd worry about me more than he already does."

"Perhaps we could visit when he's in school or out with his friends."

"He bowls every Wednesday evening."

"Then Wednesday it is."

Bishop Frost also made certain that the Everests' home teachers kept a close eye on the family. They were told about Corey's illness and were warned how sensitive he was about people knowing of his condition. The only other people in the ward who knew about Corey's illness were the Relief Society president and Mrs. Everest's visiting teachers. They dropped by often to visit Corey's mother, always bringing a flower, a thought, or a new recipe—something to let Mrs. Everest know they were thinking about her and that she had their support.

Then there was the hospice volunteer. Lynn Miller was a middle-aged woman with silver hair and a fine network of crinkles around her eyes. She worked with Mountain View Hospital helping people to cope with personal tragedies. Lynn—she never let anyone call her Sister or, heaven forbid, Mrs. Miller—was well qualified to help Mrs. Everest deal with Corey's terminal illness. Her own husband had died after a lingering bout with cancer, and her only son had died at the age of ten when he was hit by a car.

Hospice volunteers were supposed to be a source of guidance and comfort, but Lynn had quickly become more than that. She and Ruth ("If I'm to call you Lynn, then you have to call me Ruth," Mrs. Everest had told her) had become close friends. Lynn lived in Santaquin, twenty miles away, but she came to visit two or three times a week, and she phoned every day.

One morning after Corey had spent most of the night coughing and spitting up blood, Mrs. Everest called Lynn and asked her to come over. Lynn arrived twenty minutes later.

"It's just that I've had a terrible night," Mrs. Everest apologized. "Corey was so sick and I was so frightened." Lynn placed her arm around Mrs. Everest's shoulders and held her close. "It's so frightening sometimes. He spent the whole night spitting up blood, but then he went to school this morning like nothing was wrong. I don't understand it. He spends all day trying to be the human

95

firecracker, and when he comes home he's sore from arthritis, and he's sick to his stomach the next morning." She began to cry. "Sometimes I don't think he's willing to face the truth about what's happening to him. I don't want him to be miserable, but I don't feel that he's facing reality."

Lynn hugged her tightly. "He's a survivor."

"A what?"

"The term is misleading, but he's what we call a survivor. When most people are faced with tragedy, they respond by brooding, blaming others, and avoiding the problem. But survivors not only endure their challenges; they confront their stresses and sorrows in ways that enrich their lives."

"How do they do that?"

"By making happiness a habit. They treasure life and the time they have left. They take each day as it comes, looking for the flash of excitement, the moment of beauty, or the pleasure of insight. If they can't have the big victory, they happily settle for the small ones." Lynn smiled. "From what I know of Corey, that's what he's doing. He can't have the big victory, which would be full recovery, so he settles for the small ones with his friends and family."

"Then he's not simply avoiding the problem?"

"Not at all. Corey has learned an important secret. He knows that his trials are far less important than how he deals with them. You see, suffering is easy. Being happy is difficult. It takes work. And Corey knows how to make his own happiness."

She patted Mrs. Everest's hands. "I once worked with a woman suffering from bone cancer. Rather than mope and worry, she attacked life with more enthusiasm than ever before. She traveled to exotic places and made new friends. She learned new hobbies and skills." She leaned close and smiled. "She even got married."

"Married?"

"Yes! And do you know what was really amazing about that? She was seventy-five years old!"

"You're joking!"

"I'm not! But even more incredible is the fact that she was only expected to live for a matter of months. But that was five years ago, and she's still doing marvelously well."

"How?"

"No one knows. But the spirit can have a wonderful effect on the body. All I can say for certain is that she's taking one day at a time and living a wonderful life. So you see, Corey is simply dealing with the situation in the best way he knows how. And if you ask me, he's doing a wonderful job."

Mrs. Everest agreed. "He is a wonderful young man."

"And an inspiring one. I can't help but admire him for his tremendous character and attitude."

"He's given all of us a good example to follow."

• • •

There was another person who was a constant source of support and comfort. And it was someone Mrs. Everest never would have expected — Corey's father.

Mr. Everest paused to visit each time he picked Corey up for their weekly activity, and he often stopped by to check the plumbing, adjust the lawnmower, or prune the hedge. At first Mrs. Everest thought he just wanted to spend more time with Corey, but then he began arriving early in the afternoon or on Wednesday evenings when he knew Corey wouldn't be home.

They talked mostly about Corey, but sometimes they reminisced about their married life. Once they even talked about the divorce.

"It's strange," Mr. Everest admitted. "I know we struggled, but I really don't remember much about that."

"Neither do I. The more that time passes, the more I forget the bad times in favor of the good."

"We did have some wonderful times." Mr. Everest was silent for a moment. "When you first moved here, we decided to put aside our differences for Corey's sake. If we'd been intelligent enough to do that ten years ago, things would have been so much different for us."

"Different," Mrs. Everest agreed. "And better."

Chapter Thirteen

"I don't get it. I just don't get it."

Edward leaned over the engine of a rust-eaten pickup and pulled hard on a crowbar. He was tightening a belt by adjusting the position of the alternator. He wrenched down a bolt and then wiped his hands on his shirt.

"I mean, I can't even read it for one thing. And I don't understand what anybody's doing."

Javin flipped through his paperback copy of *Hamlet*. He looked over at Corey, who was reclining in a lawn chair. "It's really not that bad, Ed" Javin said. "Don't you ever watch the video in class?"

Edward looked at him with an expression that said that he wasn't in the mood for silly questions. "The movie isn't much better than the book. Still can't understand a word they say. And they all dress so much like girls that I can't tell them apart."

Javin sighed. So far Edward was keeping up with his spelling, and although he didn't see much use for it, he was even making some progress with the poetry memorization list. But trying to get Edward to understand Shakespeare was like trying to instruct a five-year-old in integral calculus.

He tried again. "Look, Ed. With most books, you read them and *then* you try to understand what you've read. But with Shakespeare, first you try to figure out what's going on, and then you know what's happening when you read it."

Edward frowned. "That don't make sense."

"This is school, Ed. It doesn't have to make sense."

Corey had been feeling tired all day, and he became dizzy if he stood up for too long, but now he was enjoying watching Javin struggle to teach Edward. He spoke up for the first time. "You ever watch TV, Ed?"

"Sometimes."

"You remember a show called 'The A Team'?"

"Yeah. They'd shoot ten thousand bullets, smash up half a dozen cars, and blow up fifteen buildings. But nobody'd ever get killed."

Corey laughed. "I never thought of that. You remember Murdock?"

"Yeah."

"What was he like?"

"He was always acting like he was crazy."

"But was he really nutso?"

"No, he was just pretending."

"Why?"

"He didn't want folks to understand him. The loonier he acted, the less people worried about him."

"Well, that's Hamlet to a T. He tries to make everybody think he's crazy, even though he's not."

"Just like Murdock?"

"Just like Murdock. Now, have you ever seen 'Dallas'?"

Edward nodded vigorously. "Yeah. It's great."

"Okay, good. Tell me about J. R."

"J. R.'s the best. He's sneaky. And mean. And he's always using people to get stuff."

Corey spread his hands. "That's just what Claudius the king is like. See, Hamlet's father was the real king, and

Claudius is Hamlet's uncle. So when Hamlet's father dies, Claudius marries Gertrude, the queen — Hamlet's mother — so that *he* can become the new king."

"Why does that make him like J. R.?"

"Do you know how the king died?"

"Didn't Claudius kill him?"

"Right! And then, even though it was forbidden by the church, he married Gertrude — just two months after the king's funeral."

"That *does* sound like something J. R. would do."

Javin jumped into the conversation. "Okay. What about Gertrude? Who's she like?"

Corey shrugged. "What's she like?"

Edward looked at Javin expectantly. For the first time, the characters were coming to life, and he was anxious to hear more.

"Well," Javin said, "she's concerned about Hamlet, but only because she's his mother. And she doesn't worry about her marriage to Claudius, even though she knows it's wrong. She's ruled by her passions."

Corey looked from Edward to Javin and then back to Edward again. "All right. Think hard. Who does that remind you of?"

"Hot Lips on 'M*A*S*H'?"

"How about Carla on 'Cheers'?"

The three boys laughed as they pictured both Hot Lips and Carla playing the part of Gertrude on the video Mrs. Hazelboom showed the class. Then they thought up TV characters to represent most of the other characters in the play and laughed for several minutes when Javin gave the parts of Rosencrantz and Guildenstern to the brothers Darryl and Darryl on "Newhart." When they discussed the basic plot of the play, Edward liked the idea of the ghost so much that he made Javin read that part for him while he worked. Corey brought certain parts of the story to life by asking, "Now, what would Murdock do in a situation like that?"

Later, after Edward and Javin had finished work and closed up the shop for the day, Corey brought up another subject.

"You ever been to a seminary dance, Ed?"

"Never been to a dance."

"Why not?"

"Just never have."

"Well, the seminary's having a dance Friday night. Why don't you come?"

"You're kidding, right?"

Corey just looked at him. Edward sighed. Like everybody else, he was learning that no matter how ridiculous one of Corey's suggestions might seem, he was never kidding.

"I can't dance —"

"Neither can I. But I'm going. Nice place to meet girls, Ed."

"That's another thing. There's no girls who'd dance with me."

"That's where you're wrong, Ed. You've just got to give yourself a chance."

"Yeah, right."

"Oh, come on, Ed. You'd have a great time."

"There's no girls in this school who'd dance with me. They all think I'm weird."

"You know what's wrong with you, Ed? You're so convinced you're a loser that you never try to do anything about it."

"Yeah, like there's really a whole lot I *can* do about it."

Corey stopped and jabbed a finger against Edward's chest. "Let me tell you something, bud. You're an okay guy. I think so, and so does Javin. The only problem is *you* don't believe it. You think you're a loser. You don't think you've got a single thing in this world going for you. Am I right?"

"Close."

"You bet I am. Now let me tell you something else. In three weeks you went from straight Ds and Fs in your classes to a solid C average. You know how many kids have got the brains — not to mention the guts — to do something like that? Not many. And besides that, you and Javin have started one of the most successful auto shops in town. How many other kids in this school own their own business? Don't know? I do — not one. Now, you can go on thinking you're a waste of space for as long as you want. But one day you ought to wake up and take a good look at yourself. You've got potential. You're just too dumb to realize it."

"But — "

"No buts, Ed. The problem with you is that you won't give yourself a chance. You know something? Jeremy gave you a chance the first time he let you work on his car. Principal Harrington gave you a chance when you wanted to open the shop. Every single day kids give you a chance when they bring their cars to you. *Everybody's* willing to give you a chance but you. And if you're not willing to take a few risks once in a while, then maybe all the rest of us ought to just give up on you too."

Both Edward and Javin were standing with their mouths open. Neither of them had seen Corey so adamant about anything before. It almost seemed out of character for him. Corey just stood looking at Edward expectantly. Finally he said, "Well?"

Edward didn't know what to say. "Well, what?"

"Are you going to go to the dance with us?"

"Yeah, I'll go."

Corey grinned and slapped him on the back. He seemed his old self again. "Good job."

• • •

Corey had told Kat that Edward was coming to the dance, and she had tried to prepare herself for the experience of seeing him at a seminary activity. Even so, nothing could have prepared her for the experience of actually seeing Edward walking across the dance floor.

"My word!" she whispered to Corey. "He actually shampooed his hair!"

"That's not all. He's wearing a suit."

"It can't be his."

"It's not. Brother Sanders helped us find it for him."

Kat looked at Corey for a moment, feeling a renewed sense of respect and admiration for her friend. In all the time she'd known Edward, she never would have believed that anyone would have actually been able to talk him into attending a seminary dance. More than that, she'd never known anyone besides Corey who would have cared enough to try.

"You know, you've really done a lot for Ed."

"Well, it's not just me. Javin's helped a lot too. And you deserve some of the credit."

"Me?"

"Yes, you. You're going to be the first one to dance with him."

Kat opened her mouth and took an involuntary step backwards. "You're kidding."

Corey gazed at her with his famous you-know-better-than-that expression. He used it so often that he was becoming quite good at it. Kat glanced at Edward and took a deep breath. "Okay," she said. "Am I supposed to ask him, or what?"

"Yeah. You go over and dance with him, and I'll go find someone to relieve you."

Kat nodded and left, and Corey went looking for Emily Jacobsen, who was the president of his seminary class.

"Emily! Just the person I wanted to see."

"Oh? You've decided that you've got a crush on me, and you want to dance with me all night, right?"

Corey grinned. "You read me like a book. Actually, I have a friend who wants to dance with you. But he's kind of shy. Would you dance with him if he asks you?"

"Sure. Who is it?"

"Edweird."

Emily almost choked on her punch. "Edweird's here?"

"Yeah. He came with me." Emily looked at Corey closely to see if he was joking. She knew instantly that he wasn't. "Now he's going to ask you to dance in a minute. You *will* say yes, won't you?" He saved time by giving her his no-I'm-not-kidding gaze before she could ask the obvious question.

Emily studied Corey for a moment and then glanced across the gym. She spotted Edward right away. He was dancing with Kat Ericksen, who seemed to be having a good time. She looked back at Corey. "Okay, then. Bring him on."

• • •

Corey walked back across the dance floor, reaching Kat and Edward just as the song ended. "Hey, you two. You make a nice-looking couple."

Edward blushed. "Kat's a good dancer."

"She's the best," Corey agreed. "But you've never danced until you've danced with Emily."

Edward's mouth went dry. "Emily Jacobsen?"

"You know her?"

He nodded weakly. "She's in my geography class."

"Neat kid, isn't she?" He pointed. "She's right over there, you know. Why don't you go ask her to dance?"

Edward opened his mouth to speak, but he saw the look on Corey's face and stopped himself just in time. "Think she'd dance with me?"

"I know so. Now get going."

Edward stood gazing across the dance floor for several seconds before, after a final look at Corey, he took a deep breath and marched off across the hall. A minute later he was dancing shyly with Emily.

Kat watched them for a moment and then turned to Corey. "You're incredible."

"You know," he said, "I think you're right."

• • •

On Sunday Corey invited Edward to church. Edward couldn't make it, but he said that he'd try to come the next week. The next day, though, Corey and Kat were just sitting down to lunch when Jeremy came in with a surprise.

"Guess who came to early morning seminary today?"

Corey took a guess. "The Three Nephites?"

"No."

"John the Beloved?"

"No."

Corey gave up. "They're the only visitors that *my* class ever has. Who?"

"Edweird."

"Really?"

"Yeah. Just came right in and sat down. I went and sat by him because he didn't know what to do, but I think he had a good time. At least Brother Sanders went out of his way to make him feel welcome."

Corey nodded in satisfaction. He would have enjoyed seeing Edward singing songs during the devotional. He looked from Jeremy to Kat and then back to Jeremy again. "You know, I think there may be hope for him after all."

Chapter Fourteen

The preliminary student-body elections were conducted that Friday, narrowing the field of candidates down to two for each office. Jeremy won in the race for student-body president, along with Tom Kelly. There would be one more week of campaigning, followed by the final election the next Friday.

"Now don't worry about it," Corey counseled Jeremy as they drove home. "You've got this election wrapped up."

"I wish I could believe that," Jeremy said, rolling down the car window and letting his arm dangle outside.

"Believe me. You're practically a shoo-in."

Jeremy wasn't ready to be convinced. "I don't know," he said. "I was lucky today, but Tom carries a lot of weight. He's got a lot of friends around the school."

"So do you. Believe me. I've been talking with people. You carry a lot more influence than you think."

Jeremy glanced over and studied his friend carefully. "You wouldn't just be giving me one of your pep talks, would you?"

"Me? When would I ever do something—"

Jeremy rolled his head and laughed. "Okay, okay. I believe you."

"And you should. Just one more week of hanging up posters, wearing buttons, and giving speeches, and, well, you'll be the new student-body president of Juab High."

Jeremy laughed again. Having Corey around was like having a constant transfusion of enthusiasm. Without him — he stopped in midthought, feeling suddenly somber. Though Corey tried to cover it, it was easy to see that his health was failing. Corey didn't have the youthful energy that he'd had even a couple of weeks ago, and sometimes Jeremy would call to find that Corey had gone to bed as early as five or six o'clock.

At the bowling alley Corey tried to act as normal as he could, but it was obvious to anyone who watched him that every roll was painful for him. Jeremy wondered just how long Corey had left. Three days? Three weeks? Three months?

He suddenly changed the subject. "You know," he said, "when my parents first started having trouble with their marriage, I didn't want anyone to know about it, and I didn't want to talk about it."

"But I didn't give you much choice, did I?"

Jeremy grinned. "No, you didn't. And you know what? Talking about it with you really helped. It made me feel better. It gave me a chance to get some things off my chest, and I really appreciate what you did for me."

"So are you okay now?"

Jeremy nodded. "Yeah. Mom and Dad are really trying to work things out. We had a family council the other night, and they let me in on the whole thing. It'll take some time, but at least they're trying." He paused. "Now what about you?"

Corey looked up mildy. "What about me?"

"How are you doing?"

"Fine."

Jeremy narrowed his eyes. "I'll understand if you don't want to talk. But remember, I didn't want to talk either — until you made me."

Corey stared out the window and off into the distance where an airliner left a pair of billowy white contrails against the blue sky. "You know what really bothers me?" he asked suddenly.

"What?"

"I worry that people will forget me."

"What do you mean?"

"I'm not sure," Corey said. "But it scares me a little. I'm afraid that when I die, it'll be like I was never here. Life will go on without me, and it won't matter that I'm not here anymore." He looked at Jeremy, and his green eyes had a faraway look in them. "It's not like I want people to sit and cry over me. And I don't want a monument or anything. But — " He shook his head as he struggled to put his thoughts into words. "But I just want to feel like my life made a difference. I want to feel like maybe life will be better for someone else because I was here."

"If that's your biggest worry, then you can stop."

Corey lifted an eyelid. "What do you mean?"

"Well, I know we've only known each other for a couple of months, and I don't want to sound mushy or anything, but you're the best thing that's ever happened around here. You're the best friend I've ever had. And I know that Kat and Javin feel the same way."

"Thanks." Corey looked away. "You know what's really weird?"

"What's that?"

"People who say that death isn't anything to worry about. You've heard that, haven't you? That as long as you're righteous and obeying the commandments and every-thing, that you don't have anything to worry about?" He laughed. "That's *crazy*. I mean, I trust God and everything. There have been enough people die before me that I'm sure they've got all the bugs worked out of the system. But hey, I still worry about it. It's like when I started going to school here. I didn't know what it was going to be like."

"It's kind of like fear of the unknown, isn't it?"

"Yeah. That's it exactly. But you wouldn't believe the number of people who tell me that if I just have faith then there's nothing to worry about. I appreciate the thought, but it's like walking into a snowstorm and trying not to get cold." He rolled his eyes. "Believe me, I've been out in winter, and even with coats and caps and gloves and everything else you can think of to keep warm, there have still been times that I've managed to get cold." He was thoughtful for a moment. "You know what's cool, though?"

"What's that?"

"I had a talk with my bishop not too long ago, and he told me to think of all the people we'll get to meet on the other side — you know, friends we made before in the preexistence, and then all the famous people like Nephi and Alma and Abraham Lincoln."

"Who knows? Maybe you were friends with Nephi and Alma and Abraham Lincoln." Jeremy changed the subject. "Do you mind if I ask you something else? I mean, I know how you hate being asked the same ol' thing over and over again."

"No, go ahead."

"Well, I was just wondering why you'd want to spend the rest of your life in a place like Nephi. If it were me, boy, I'd be out sailing around the world."

"You forget," Corey said. "I've lived in Pueblo *and* Nephi, the two excitement capitals of the world. I don't need to travel. Besides, I'm a people person. I'd rather spend my time with people than things. I want to spend my time with my mom and dad — and my friends."

Jeremy nodded. "You know what you said a minute ago—about your friends on the other side?"

"Yeah."

"Well, if heaven is anything like Nephi, I think you're going to have more friends than you know what to do with."

• • •

Wednesday night was the league bowling championship. Corey wasn't feeling very well that night and bowled beneath his average, but Javin had the best night of his life, scoring more than enough points to make up for it. Jeremy and Kat both bowled well, too, giving the team enough points to take second place. Normally they would have gone straight to the Burger Barn to celebrate. But not tonight.

"I'm sorry to ruin everything for you," Corey said, "but I'm just not feeling very well. Would you mind taking me home?"

"Not at all."

They drove home in silence.

• • •

By Friday afternoon, the day of the final election, Jeremy was a nervous wreck.

"Don't worry about it," Corey told him. "It's like I said. You're a shoo-in."

"I don't know," Jeremy said. "Tom ran a pretty intense campaign."

"So did you," Corey said, trying to sound as encouraging as possible. "Now just relax. The election's over, the votes are being counted—there's nothing more you can do. So just enjoy it."

111

"Corey, if I'd just fallen into a patch of poison ivy, you'd be telling me to laugh and enjoy it."

Corey laughed and clapped a hand on Jeremy's shoulder. They left the school and began walking toward the parking lot. Jeremy waited until they wouldn't be overheard and then said, "You know, whether I win or not, this is the funnest thing I've ever done. I've made a lot of new friends, and I've got to do things I never would have otherwise. Thanks for getting me started."

"Anytime."

"No, really," Jeremy said. "If it wasn't for you, I never would have dared to run for student-body president." He grinned. "Without you I never would have dared to run for school milk monitor."

Corey just laughed. He'd got up that morning with an unsettling, queasy sensation in his stomach, and he'd felt a little dizzy all day, but he was just as excited as Jeremy about the election.

Jeremy picked up Corey, Kat, and Javin later that night and drove them back to the school for the election dance. Corey and Kat spent most of the night dancing together, though Jeremy and Javin both cut in several times.

According to the schedule, the election results were to be announced at 8:30. And the closer that time came, the more nervous Jeremy became. Still, he was trying to be a good sport. At 8:25, he went looking for Tom and shook his hand.

"Good luck," he said.

"Yeah, same to you," Tom said.

Jeremy mustered up the biggest smile he could come up with under the circumstances. "I had a good time running against you."

A few minutes later the student council turned off the music and called for attention. Then, one by one, they began naming the winners of each office. And just as people always did at school elections, they drew out each announcement as long as possible to heighten the suspense. They introduced the new secretary, vice president, and president of the junior class and then did the same thing for the senior class.

Jeremy whispered to Kat, "I don't know how much more of this I can stand." Kat just squeezed his arm in reply.

Finished with the class officers, the student council began announcing the new student-body officers. They announced the school historian, secretary, publicity chairperson, news reporter, and radio announcer. Then, finally, they announced the student-body secretary and the student-body vice president.

"And now," the student-body president said, "for the moment we've all been waiting for—the new student-body president." He waited until the school gym was perfectly silent and then said, "But first let me read a few thoughts."

He released a roll of paper that unrolled for about thirty feet across the floor. Everyone groaned. The president grinned as though he had just performed the most original joke in history and then turned back to the microphone. "The new president of Juab High School is—Jeremy Falkner!"

Jeremy jumped in the air, and then he threw his arms around Kat and hugged her wildly. People were throwing confetti in the air and shouting, "Jer-a-my! Jer-a-my! Jer-a-my!" The noise was so loud that it was almost impossible to speak as Jeremy pushed his way through the crowd to the front of the gym. Everyone was clapping and shouting at the top of their lungs.

Everyone but Corey.

As soon as Corey had jumped up from the bench, a wave of dizziness hit him with such force that he'd had to sit back down. He suddenly felt sick to his stomach. He looked around in a moment of panic, knowing that more than anything he needed fresh air. He pulled himself to his feet and staggered from the gym. Everyone was so involved watching Jeremy that no one even saw Corey leave.

• • •

Corey sat down heavily on the cold concrete steps outside the gym, breathing deeply. He thought that the night air would clear his head, but it didn't. He felt as dizzy as if he'd just crawled off the Zip-O-Wheel at the county fair, and his stomach was churning. It was getting harder to breathe.

"Corey? Is that you?"

Corey looked up, but his vision blurred, and he couldn't see who it was.

"Corey? What's wrong, man?"

The voice finally registered. "Ed . . . Ed, bud?"

"Yeah. What's wrong, man?"

Corey had to place a hand over his stomach, and it was several seconds before he could answer. "I'm sick, Ed. Really, really sick. You've . . . got to help me."

"Sure. Anything. Just tell me what you want me to do."

Corey was breathing rapidly now, trying to fill his lungs with air. His lungs flamed in his chest and he felt as if he were drowning.

"Call my mom . . . and my dad." He breathed deeply and suffered the frightening sensation of not being able to catch his breath. "Then . . . then you've got to get me to . . . the hospital."

Chapter Fifteen

The smell of antiseptic filled the hospital room with a smell that was sticky sweet. The curtains to the only window were drawn wide open, revealing a brilliant, sunsoaked world outside that seemed oblivious to the gloom inside the hospital.

Corey was sitting up in bed, supported by what looked like a dozen different pillows. He was wearing a thin, tired smile, though his face was drawn and pale. Looking at him, Kat thought he seemed different, almost as if something bright and cheerful had been drained from him. Even his eyes seemed pale and washed out.

Even so, Corey had not lost his sense of humor. "I don't understand it," he rasped. "If they really wanted to keep me here, you'd think they'd treat me better. So far they haven't done anything but stick me with needles and fill me with tubes." He grimaced as though something, somewhere, suddenly hurt.

"How's the food?" Javin asked, not able to come up with anything more original to say.

"It's okay," Corey said, "but after a couple of days it all starts to taste the same. I know you won't believe this, but right now even the thought of school lunch makes my mouth water."

Javin's eyes lit up. "Hey, we could bring you one. We could smuggle it in a box."

"You want to feed school lunch to a sick person?" Jeremy asked. He shook his head. "Bad idea. We don't want to kill him."

Kat looked at Jeremy sharply, but Corey quickly spoke up, apparently unconcerned. "How would you guys like to do me a favor?"

"Sure," Kat said, happy to have the topic changed. "Anything."

Corey looked at Jeremy. "You remember when I told you that I didn't want to go around the world sightseeing and looking at things?"

"Yeah."

Corey shifted on his bed, uncomfortable despite all the pillows. "Well, being in the hospital for the past five days has been a real drag. And there is one thing that I'd like to see again."

"What is it?"

"Alpenglow."

Jeremy and Javin looked at each other. "Alpenglow? What's that?"

Corey gasped for breath and then quickly composed himself. "It's something you see in the mountains just before it gets dark," he said. "Kat can tell you all about it." He struggled again to catch his breath. "What I'd like is for you three to take me up the canyon. I kinda miss it."

Kat spoke up softly. "Are you sure that's such a good idea?"

Corey nodded. "Yeah. It really would make me feel better."

"But will they let you go?"

Corey managed his best let-'em-just-try-and-stop-me shrug. "Sure."

Just as Corey's friends feared, the hospital staff didn't want to let Corey out of sight. But—as Jeremy once phrased it—arguing with Corey was like arguing with a supreme court judge. Or a four-star general. You just couldn't win.

So that afternoon the four teenagers drove out of town in Jeremy's Mustang—Corey insisted on that, too—and up the canyon.

"Look at all the shades of green," Corey whispered when they finally found a spot high in the hills and parked. He had already explained the mysteries of alpenglow to Jeremy and Javin, and they were both anxious to experience it. "I think I love pine trees more than anything," Corey continued.

Kat eased up to his side and put an arm around him. "Why is that?"

"Because they're always green. Even in winter, when other trees turn brown and seem to die, the pines stay green." He paused long enough to catch his breath. "It's like they're always alive and always cheerful." He looked at each of his friends in turn. "I hope people will remember me like that."

They all sat on the grass and passed the time talking quietly.

"Moroni," Corey said.

"What?"

"Moroni. I'd like to meet Moroni someday."

"Me too," Jeremy said, remembering the time they'd talked about people they'd like to meet in the spirit world. "And Joseph Smith." He thought for a moment. "I'd like to meet John Taylor and Brigham Young, too."

Corey looked at Kat. "How about you? If you could visit the spirit world, who would you like to meet?"

"Eliza R. Snow. She was incredible."

117

Corey nodded thoughtfully. "Yeah. I'd like to meet her too. And George Washington. I've always liked him." He looked at Javin. "How about you?"

Javin didn't hesitate. "Hamlet."

Everybody looked at him and frowned. "Hamlet? Why?"

"To find out if he was really crazy."

Everybody laughed. It was like Javin to pick a person no one else would have thought of.

Corey coughed to clear his throat. "When you get on the other side, I wonder if they let you go around and meet people?"

"I don't know why not," Jeremy said. "In fact, you might even get to do missionary work with them."

Corey's eyes lit up. "Wouldn't that be awesome? Getting to be missionary companions with Ammon or Alma?"

"Do you suppose that's possible?" Kat asked.

"Who knows? Maybe they're all up there doing work like General Authorities. But on the other hand, why not?"

The sun gradually sank into the west as they talked, finally dropping beneath the craggy mountain rims in the distance. A moment later, Corey whispered, "Look."

The mountains were suddenly awash in a soft, orange glow, and for a moment Corey seemed his old self. His face radiated the youthful energy that his friends had come to admire, and his eyes danced and sparkled.

And then, almost before any of them realized it, it was dark.

• • •

Jeremy, Kat, and Javin were each at the hospital again late the next day. They were visiting quietly in the foyer when Mrs. Everest walked in. Corey's dad and Bishop Frost were with her.

"We've come to give Corey a blessing," the bishop said. He glanced at Mr. Everest. "Perhaps Jeremy and Javin would like to join us." Mr. Everest lifted his eyebrows in a gesture of invitation. Jeremy and Javin both nodded.

Corey was barely awake. He didn't move when the visitors entered the room, but his eyes slid slowly back and forth as he looked at each of his friends. Mr. Everest knelt beside him and whispered to him for a moment, then gestured for the bishop, who anointed Corey with consecrated oil. Then they placed their hands on his head, as did Jeremy and Javin.

It was a beautiful prayer. Kat half hoped to hear Mr. Everest use the power of the priesthood to command his son to be made whole, but he only spoke words of love and comfort. Even so, there came a feeling in the room that Kat had never known before. It filled her with a sense of courage. And at that moment she knew more powerfully than she ever had in her life that her Father in Heaven lived. She knew without question that he loved her, and that he loved Corey, and that he was listening to that prayer. She knew without doubt that everything was going to be okay.

• • •

Over the next few days, Corey gradually regained strength. He was able to sit up in bed, and even though breathing was difficult for him, he was able to talk in a soft, raspy whisper. By the end of the week, he was strong enough to insist that his mother take him home.

Again, the hospital staff argued, but Corey would just listen and smile and say, "If that's all you've got to say, I really would like to go home now."

Mr. and Mrs. Everest loaded him into the van on a Sunday evening and drove him home.

"It's good to be back," Corey said as he lay back in his own bed. "I don't ever want to leave." He closed his eyes for a moment and sighed, then looked at his parents. They were holding hands. Corey's eyes widened, and a grin spread across his face. "Two little lovers, sittin' in a tree — "

His mother blushed, and his father placed an arm around her. "We've been seeing things a little differently lately," he said simply.

Corey nodded. "I had a feeling about you two."

• • •

Corey woke up the next night unable to catch his breath. His father, sleeping in the living room on the couch, immediately wanted to call an ambulance, but Corey stopped him.

"No, Dad. Please, don't. I don't want to leave."

"But Corey — "

Corey took his father's hand and squeezed it. "Please, Dad."

Mr. Everest stayed by his son for the rest of the night. Corey eventually fell asleep, but it was not a restful sleep. He tossed and turned and occasionally woke up gasping for breath. Mrs. Everest had to leave the room for a while. She couldn't bear to see her son suffering so much. But by the time the sun came up the next morning, he wasn't suffering anymore.

Chapter Sixteen

The ward chapel was filled to capacity. Students from school packed the padded benches until the curtains leading into the cultural hall were opened to provide for an overflow. Many of them wept openly. Except for Jeremy, Kat, and Javin, no one had even known that Corey was sick, and his death had come as a shock.

The funeral was kept simple. Brother Sanders spoke about death and resurrection, quoting scriptures from the Old and New Testaments, the Doctrine and Covenants, and the Book of Mormon. When he finished, four girls from Corey's seminary class sang a song.

And then Jeremy spoke. "Not too long ago, Corey told me that he wanted to make a difference in this life. He wanted to feel that he had been important in the lives of the people he knew." He gazed around the crowded chapel. "Well, I want you to know that he made a difference in my life. He gave me the confidence to do things I never would have tried on my own. He helped me to see the best in myself when I could only see the worst. He helped me through some rough times."

Jeremy was trying to keep his emotions under control,

but he felt his eyes beginning to well with tears, and he felt a lump rising in his throat.

"Corey loved pine trees," he said. "He said that even in winter, when other trees became brown and appeared to die, the pines stayed green and beautiful. And I think Corey was a lot like that. Even though he faced an illness that he knew would take his life, he never quit thinking about his friends. Even though the problems he faced were more serious than anything we can realize, he never dwelled on them. Instead, he went out of his way to make the rest of us happy. He spent the last months of his life serving others."

Jeremy tried to fight back the tears. His voice was little more than a whisper. "At first, I wondered how I would ever get along without Corey. He was like a battery charger to me, and he changed my life. I wondered how I would ever get by without that." He looked up. "But you know, Corey hasn't done anything for us that we can't do for ourselves. And I want to promise you that I'm going to follow his example.

"John Taylor said: 'It is true, we do not like to lose a friend, but we have to do it, and it is right and proper that we should. They go a little before us; when we get there they will receive and welcome us. I expect to strike hands and embrace my friends who have gone before.' "

Jeremy had more to say, but suddenly he couldn't say any more. He stood for nearly a minute while the tears flowed freely down his face.

Bishop Frost, who was conducting the service, stood and hugged him. Then he turned to the microphone. "I think it would be most appropriate if everyone stood and joined hands."

He waited as the congregation formed a giant chain that extended not only through the chapel but also through the cultural hall and both foyers. Then Javin offered the closing prayer.

After the burial many people returned to the church, where they stayed for several hours, hugging and weeping and expressing their feelings.

Finally, Jeremy found Kat and Javin. "Let's go for a drive," he suggested. "Up the canyon."

They were leaving the building when Kat put a hand on Jeremy's arm. Jeremy turned to see Kat pointing to the far side of the cultural hall, where, way in the back and off by himself, Edward was sitting in a folding chair. He held a hymnbook open on his lap, but he wasn't reading it.

Jeremy glanced at Kat and Javin and then stepped quickly across the room. "Hi, Ed."

Edward looked up slowly, his eyes reflecting no emotion. Jeremy cleared his throat. "We're going for a ride up the canyon," he said, nodding toward Kat and Javin. "Like to come?"

Edward looked at him for a moment, then nodded once. "Yeah," he said, "I would."

The four teenagers rode up the canyon in silence, lost in thought. After driving for several miles, Jeremy turned onto a side road and parked on a knoll that overlooked a scenic backcountry canyon filled with pine trees. Without speaking, they left the car and sat in the grass. The sun was just touching the craggy mountain rims in the west, streaking the sky with rays of fiery red and brilliant orange.

Kat squinted at the many different shades of green in the distance, trying to find one that matched the color of Corey's eyes. Most were too dark, and many were too light. None were exactly right. Even so, she knew she would never experience a mountain sunset without thinking of him.

Jeremy touched her lightly on the arm, and without turning, she knew what he wanted.

It was alpenglow.